Gray Goo

DISCLAIMER

This book is a work of fiction. Names, characters, businesses, places, events, locales, and incidents are either the products of the author's imagination or used in a fictitious manner. Any resemblance to actual persons, living or dead, or actual events or locales is purely coincidental.

The places described in this book do not exist and any similarity to real world locations is unintentional and not meant to be taken literally. The author and publisher take no responsibility for any misunderstandings that may arise from this fictional presentation. The views and opinions expressed in this book are those of the fictional characters and do not necessarily reflect those of the author, the publisher, or any other person or entity. Any description of actions, behaviors, or conditions is intended solely for the purpose of storytelling and should not be taken as endorsement, guidance, or recommendation.

Readers are advised to suspend their belief in the world as they know it and immerse themselves in the realm of the imagination as they turn the pages of this book. All laws of reality, as we know them, may be broken or reshaped at the whim of the author for the entertainment of the readers.

To my wife Jessica,

This book is dedicated to you. Thank you for putting up with me during the writing process and for your invaluable help during the editing process. This book wouldn't be nearly as good without your insight.

Love,
Devin

Gray Goo - *A speculative catastrophe wherein unchecked self-replicating nanomachines consume all matter, resulting in a uniformly lifeless world. This term encapsulates not a physical condition, but a bleak potential future devoid of the rich diversity of life as we know it today.*

Introduction

The night sky was still and cloudless above the quiet town of Bridgefield; the stars twinkled peacefully, creating a soft glow in the thin air. The infinite black void of space was interrupted when a blinding beam pierced the abyss like a shooting star. This was the first ship to arrive. Cigar-shaped, it glided through the darkness with grace. Its hull was smooth and unblemished, the celestial dome reflecting off it like a mirror. Once the ship had maneuvered into position, it rotated swiftly before becoming eerily still, suspending itself in the night sky as it awaited the arrival of the second craft. A profound silence cloaked the vessel, underlining its alien nature amid the familiar nocturnal ambiance. The only audible sound was the subtle whisper of the crisp high-altitude breeze, a gentle rustling interrupting the otherwise silent night.

The silence was shattered with a boom when the second craft arrived, again a burst of light shot across the sky. This craft seemed more crude than the first, it made noise as it traveled and had four large fin-like panels protruding from each side. It glowed red as it entered Earth's atmosphere, leaving a fiery trail in its wake. The hostility between these ships became apparent when the more advanced one began to fire energy beams at the second. The second ship did not react in any way to being fired upon and was hit with two large blasts. The second ship tumbled towards Earth aflame and crashed in a dramatic explosion. Silently, the more advanced silver cigar lowered itself towards the crash site, landing about a mile away next to some industrial buildings.

Once on the ground, the silver exterior began to shake violently, and a loud grinding noise filled the quiet desolate streets. The noise bounced off the large factories and warehouses. In a matter of seconds, the sleek spacecraft had transformed. The metal had twisted, folded, and morphed until the almost perfect ovoid mirror had molded itself into an old, rusted bus, complete with black tinted windows and peeling paint. The bus sat motionless next to a pile of trash. The night sky once again returned to its peaceful state, as if nothing had happened. The quiet town of Bridgefield remained oblivious to the strange events that had just occurred above them, and life carried on as usual.

A hundred miles away a computer screen flashed with a warning, "Two assets detected: Location 41.6404344, -72.6343060"

A slender brunette with a sharp jawline sat at her desk. She wore a tight-fitting blazer and skirt, she took a sip from her early morning coffee as she inspected the notice. Her back faced the lights from New York's skyline, glittering in the backdrop of her high-rise. Her face creased into a frown as she read the message.

"Why there, of all places?" she mumbled, quickly grabbing her cell phone to contact her boss.

"You seeing this sir?"

"Yes," he replied in a stern voice, "how soon can you leave?"

"As soon as possible."

"Good. Depart now, the team will meet you there. Dina, are you certain you can handle this?"

With confidence in her voice, she assured him. "Yes, I'll be fine. Sir, I won't let you down."

CHAPTER 1 - THE GRIND

The morning sun peeked through the window blinds of Jack's small apartment, casting a warm glow on his haggard face. Jack rented a quaint studio in the solitary apartment complex of Bridgefield, a town that seemed to exist in the margins of memory. This small and unassuming community, largely forgotten by the world, found itself nestled inconspicuously between the bustling metropolitan behemoths of New York and Boston.

Jack groaned as he began to awaken. The stale odor of cigarettes, sweat, and old Chinese food made him gag. His first thought was how to cure the head throbbing from the remnants of last night's heroin high. He opened one eye and rolled his head to the side, glancing at the clock on the nightstand: 7 A.M. Thursday. Jack released a long sigh unconsciously, to express the disappointment with life's monotony. He swung his legs over the edge of the bed and just sat for a minute.

Next to the bed was a large dresser with a mirror on top. The top of the dresser was cluttered with the mistakes of nights past. He looked over the contents and without the gloss from the drugs the chaotic nature of his home was unmistakable. The clutter was a mixture of takeout containers and beer cans. There was a scattered array of drug paraphernalia. A photograph of Jack's mother sat up amongst the mess; her happy face was in stark contrast to the grim reality.

Jack got up and shuffled to the bathroom sink, kicking an old pizza box on the way. He looked in the mirror and took mental note of the damage he had done to himself. The bags under the eyes were becoming more apparent as each day passed. The cheeks were sunken in from malnutrition. He wondered how much longer he could hide this addiction from his family. He couldn't imagine the heartbreak such knowledge would cause them. They haven't seen him in some time, but the excuses were beginning to run out. You can only be "called into work last minute" so many times before people start asking questions. He was one wrong move away from being one of those guys that stands at the crosswalk holding up signs that read "will work for food".

He was once into fitness, and making something of himself. Jack went to college and was studying chemical engineering, but a bad car accident got him hooked on oxycodone. His prescription eventually ran out but his pain remained. This over time turned into a heroin addiction; his hopes and dreams only felt like a distant memory. Jack brushed his teeth and splashed some water in his face. He looked in the mirror again, his bloodshot eyes stared back at him, his hands trembled. He grabbed a small baggy from the counter and took a small bump, not even to get high, just to get normal.

Jack had so far refused to inject the opiates despite him knowing the high would be better. To Jack this is the last shred of decency he had left. However, despite the sorry state Jack is in now this isn't a story about addiction or recovery. The state of his life was just the catalyst for why he was so desperate. It's why he was pretty much willing to try anything to turn his life around. The question is, at what cost?

After he got ready, Jack was picked up by a coworker. They were on their way to the factory. He hated working there. The incessant hum of the machinery drove him mad. He went through the motions of his workday, plotting the next time he could get his fix. He still had some in his pocket and wondered if the boss would get suspicious if he snuck off again. He felt like a prisoner in his own body. He was stuck in between reality and what helped him escape it.

Sometimes, Jack fantasized about overdosing. At least he would die with a bang rather than a whimper. That sweet numb, warm, nothingness, like a hug from the universe itself. Jack had tried other drugs in the past but nothing sunk its teeth into him quite like this. The real problem was the way he felt about life in general. In the depths of Jack's mind, a thought surfaced - maybe if he had something to work towards, he might find the strength to become sober. But then a counter-thought arose, clean for what? To mindlessly press buttons in this soulless factory?

Jack looked across the conveyor belt and saw his future sitting in front of him. It was his coworker who was fifty-five. He started at the factory the same age Jack was now. In 30 years, he had shifted down the line approximately 10 feet. Jack imagined the buttons that he got to push. He imagined how his fingerprints were permanently embedded in them. The only thing he had to show for all the years of service was a small red pin clipped to his shirt and a fifty-cent pay bump from the money Jack makes now. The years of stagnation were visible, as his arms had begun to shrivel. He noticed Jack looking at him and hit him with a classic line, "Having fun yet?"

It was a rhetorical question, just something to say to pass the time. Jack started to get nauseous at the thought that people like this existed. Worse off, that one day he could very well become one of them. He thought of how he would probably kill himself if he was completely sober and had to listen to the unrelenting clatter of the machines. As the day dragged on, his desperation grew. He couldn't keep living this way; he needed a change. But he didn't know how to make it happen. He was stuck in his addiction, his life, and he didn't see a way out.

Jack's train of thought was abruptly halted by a vibration in his pocket. It was a text message from Dave, a name he hadn't seen on his phone screen for over a month.

"Sup bro, long time no see, wanna catch up?"

He hesitated for a moment, his thumb hovering over the reply button. The temptation to escape from the monotony of his life was overwhelming. Jack was also curious about Dave's whereabouts and what he'd been doing. Dave, like Jack, was also a twenty-five-year-old worker at the factory, whose life had been derailed by an unfortunate incident. They would often crack inside jokes to one another at the expense of the old guys who always were giving them a hard time. However, Dave had mysteriously disappeared about a month ago, no longer showing up for work. Jack had assumed he'd moved on or found another job, but it was strange that Dave hadn't mentioned anything.

However a couple of days ago, as Jack stood in the checkout line after grocery shopping, he was shocked to see Dave on the front cover of a magazine. Dave was pulling off a skateboarding trick that Jack didn't recognize, but it was clear that it was no simple feat. Even more puzzling was Dave's physical condition. The last time Jack had seen him, Dave was limping, a consequence of a severe skateboarding accident he'd had years ago.

Dave wasn't tall, just about 5' 9", with long hair that made him look as though he'd washed up on a beach. His nonchalant attitude was constant, making it seem like he didn't have a care in the world. Jack knew bits and pieces of his past, mainly that he had once been a passionate skateboarder. After breaking his leg while attempting a complex trick at a major event, his prospects of a professional skateboarding career had vanished. Dave had waited too long to get his leg treated, resulting in a permanent limp. His skills had deteriorated since the accident, leaving him unable to perform at a level that could have potentially transformed his life.

Jack's attention shifted back to his phone, his mind still filled with confusion. He quickly typed out a response, "Sure, how about Olympia Diner? I'll be off work in an hour." Olympia Diner was a local establishment, known for its conducive environment for conversation, unlike the noisy bar.

As he sat in the passenger seat of his coworker's truck, making his way towards the diner, a growing unease began to overshadow his initial anticipation. He couldn't shake the feeling that something was off about this meeting. It struck him as peculiar, that despite frequently interacting with drug dealers, he now felt nervous about meeting a friend. Nevertheless, as the diner came into view, he brushed aside his unease, attributing it to his typical junky paranoia.

Jack stepped out of the truck, his co-worker pulled over by the side of the road near the entrance to the diner's parking lot. As he made his way towards the diner, his eyes caught sight of Franklin, leaning against the wall. Franklin was his drug dealer, an intimidating figure who used his position to bully his clients. Jack despised dealing with him due to his imposing stature and unpredictable nature. Franklin always seemed to be the tallest person in any room, and he would often use that to his advantage.

"What's up, creampuff?" Franklin called out mockingly.

"Fuck," Jack muttered under his breath, cringing at being spotted. A familiar tingle of fear ran up his spine.

"Hey, Franklin, just trying to get some food," Jack replied, striving to sound non-confrontational as he continued his march towards the door. Franklin glared at him.

"Remember, you still owe me from last week."

"I told you, I get paid on Friday. You'll get your money," Jack retorted, the sharpness of his response surprising even himself. As he closed the gap between them, he could feel Franklin's intense gaze burning into him like a spotlight. The neon sign above the diner bathed Franklin's face in a menacing, blood-red glow. He said nothing, just scowled as Jack passed.

A wave of relief washed over Jack once he stepped inside the diner, feeling momentarily safe from Franklin's scrutiny. The aroma of frying bacon filled the air, accompanied by the comforting sizzle of food on the griddle.

Inside, Jack spotted Dave sitting in the back corner, strategically positioned away from potential eavesdroppers. Dave appeared different than Jack remembered - more polished and put-together. He still carried his surfer style, but his clothes were newer, his overall appearance like a car freshly waxed. Gone was the skinny kid with long, greasy hair and clothing marred by cigarette burns and holes from skateboarding falls. This version of Dave seemed transformed, as if he'd gained 20 pounds of muscle in the past month. His outfit was clearly designer, adorned with a large, eye-catching graphic.

As Jack moved forward, Dave's face lit up with a broad grin.

"Bro, it's been too long!" he exclaimed.

He rose from his seat and embraced Jack in a warm hug, his scent surprisingly devoid of stale cigarette smoke. They settled into the booth, facing each other.

"You look amazing," Jack started.

"You look like shit," Dave shot back.

Dave wasn't wrong. Jack was still grimy from the day's labor, and the high from the bump he'd taken in the factory bathroom which was beginning to wear off. Next to Dave's newly fit physique, Jack looked skeletal. The diner's overhead lighting accentuated his hollowed cheeks, a stark reminder of the decline since Dave last saw him. However, Jack appreciated Dave's blunt honesty. He did look terrible, a fact both of them acknowledged with a shared laugh.

"Okay, what the fuck is the secret?" Jack began, curiosity brimming in his eyes. "I mean, you look like a different person."

Dave, grinning ear to ear, replied, "If I just flat out told you, you wouldn't believe me. Fuck, I can barely believe it myself. This past month has been crazy."

Jack, drawn in by Dave's enthusiasm, responded, "Dude, my life sucks right now. I'm willing to believe just about anything."

Dave let out a hearty laugh, knowing full well the truth in Jack's statement. He paused as the waitress approached to take their orders and set down two glasses of water.

Once the waitress was gone, Dave leaned in, his tone more serious than usual. "Ok, I'll just start from the beginning. Don't talk, just let me tell the whole story, and I'll answer any questions after."

Jack nodded, leaning back in his seat. "Okay," he said, taking a sip of his water.

Dave started his story, "About a month ago, I went to the bar."

Jack knew immediately which bar Dave was referring to, given that there was only one in town.

Dave continued, "I'll usually get pretty hammered when I go out, but this night I went a little off the rails. Now when I get drunk, like really drunk, I don't know why but I have a habit of just wanting to skateboard."

Jack interjected, a smirk on his face, "Naturally."

Jack was familiar with this habit of Dave's from their numerous nights out together. Dave's disappearance, followed by his return half an hour later with an assortment of injuries, was a common occurrence.

Dave gave him a grin to acknowledge the remark then continued, "So I grab my board and leave the bar. Now I'm cruising along and get this crazy idea, tonight's the night, I'm bombing Nook's Hill"

Jack knew bombing meant going down the hill at full speed, when he heard this he had to cut in, "Wait, wait, wait, you bombed Nook's Hill, bombed?"

"Bro, just listen, but yes I bombed Nook's Hill, bombed. They had just paved that shit and it was too good to pass up. Let me tell you it was intense, now I bet if I was sober I coulda done it but about halfway down I started to get the speed wobbles. I totally bailed and hit the pavement hard. It was probably the hardest fall that I have taken since the accident that fucked my leg up, it was gnarly. So anyway, my board at this point is gone and I'm all banged up. I mean, I had road rash all over my arms and legs and I was still super drunk and my board was gone, it was bogus. Okay, so this is the important part. I was all beat up at this point and I just wanted a place to regroup, that's when I saw this bus. Like an old abandoned school bus parked down at the bottom of the hill and I noticed the door was open."

Dave looked around to make sure no one was around to listen and his voice got quieter.

"So this bus was totally abandoned, like it was all old and rusted so I figured no one would mind if I used it to pop a squat. Well, I went inside and this was no normal bus. As soon as I was inside it was like I was in a laboratory. Like all the seats in the bus were taken out and just all this scientific looking shit was inside. But it had a bed in the middle like maybe it was a medical bus or something. I didn't know what was going on. Also, mind you, I was still fucked up, I mean I really staggered into this thing. But I

18

figured I would lay down on the bed since the seats were gone. Now this is where things got weird, and I must admit my memory is a bit shaky. Anyway, as I started to fall asleep I felt a poke in my stomach and I opened my eyes to see a robot arm stabbing me with a fucking massive needle. Like a really big ass needle. So I totally freaked out and ran home and passed out. When I woke up the next day I thought the whole thing was a dream but it wasn't and ever since I got that injection I have never felt better in my life. Like I don't know what that shit was but it must have been like stem cells or some experimental shit because I feel fantastic. So what do you think?"

Dave held his arms out like someone who had just performed a magic trick, waiting for applause.

Jack's face was completely blank, mirroring the expression of someone waiting for a punchline that never came. He realized that Dave was serious. This realization worried Jack, making him question Dave's sanity.

The pair fell silent for a bit, each just looking at the other from across the table. Dave could see the confusion and worry in Jack's eyes. The waitress returned with their food. They each thanked her and took their plates.

After the waitress walked away, Dave said, "Ok, listen. I'm gonna take a leak, then we will eat and I'm sure by then you will have had some time to think."

Dave slid out of the booth and walked to the bathroom. Jack glanced over as he walked away. Dave's stride was smooth and even, showing no evidence of the limp that used to plague him. Jack was stunned; this was a problem that even doctors couldn't fix. This limp wasn't just due to improper bone setting, but also nerve damage.

Just before Dave entered the bathroom, he glanced back at Jack and gave a subtle smirk. Jack simply shook his head from side to side and smiled. It was too good to be true.

Jack looked out the diner window and saw Franklin standing outside. Franklin was saying goodbye to some thug buddies of his. They all got into a flashy looking car, and Franklin got into his truck to drive away - clearly the conclusion to a business transaction.

Jack reached into his pocket and pulled out a bag of powder. Dave was in the bathroom and Jack was alone in the corner of the room, so he seized the opportunity. He dipped his key into the bag and took a quick bump, then stowed the contraband back in his pocket. He could feel his nerves starting to settle, but the act left him feeling dirty.

Dave emerged from the bathroom and walked back to the table. Jack quickly wiped his nose. Dave sat back down and gave Jack a suspicious look. Without saying anything, the two began to eat their food.

By the end of his meal, Jack had mulled over Dave's story.

"Ok, Dave, I'll bite. Honestly, I don't have much to lose."

Dave laughed then said, "Yeah, man, I know it's a trip and I know it's hard to believe, but it's what happened."

"Ya know, I think you're fucking crazy, right?" Dave laughed, fully aware that if he were in Jack's shoes, he'd probably think the same.

"Listen, my life has been a wild roller coaster for the past month, but it has actually made things better for me overall. I don't know what's up with this bus or whatever it is, but I just drove by, and it's still there. Maybe it's some experiment from the university or perhaps the government is testing something, I can't say for sure. What I do know is that this thing has completely transformed my life. And let's face it, your life sucks big time. I mean, have you even looked at yourself lately? Not to be a downer, buddy, but you look like the crypt keeper."

Jack looked down, admitting, "Yeah, I know I've really let myself go."

"This thing could truly fix your shit, and we could go check it out right now. I mean, how much longer can you keep up with this sorry excuse for a life?"

Jack still wasn't entirely convinced, but he figured there was no harm in taking a look.

"Fine, show me this bus. It'll be fun to see this thing and discover it's just an ordinary bus. And when it turns out to be a normal bus, you owe me a beer."

Dave smiled, sealing the deal. "Deal! Let's go. I'll drive."

Dave left some money on the table to cover both of their meals, and Jack didn't object to the kind gesture. They got up and hopped into Dave's new car. The drive wasn't too far, and they reminisced like old times on their way to Nook's Hill.

CHAPTER 2 - THE BUS

The car came to a halt at the bottom of Nooks Hill. During after-work hours, the industrial park area appeared desolate. It took a moment for Jack to spot the bus amidst the rusted debris and crushed cinder blocks. The tires were flat, sunk nearly up to the frame in mud. The bus itself seemed long retired, with flaking paint and a thick layer of rust. The windows were obscured by a dense fog, concealing what lay inside. Dave, brimming with excitement, pointed at the bus and exclaimed, "See, I told you I wasn't crazy!"

"We'll see, Dave," Jack replied, his tone monotonous and skeptical.

They stepped out of the car and walked towards the bus. Dave's enthusiasm was palpable, even though he himself had difficulty fully believing his own story.

Jack followed along, maintaining his skeptical demeanor. As they entered the bus, Jack had to hunch over due to the limited headroom, while Dave could stand up straight. Jack began to survey his surroundings and quickly realized that Dave was right—this bus was anything but ordinary.

The control panel for driving didn't resemble any bus he had seen before. Instead of a traditional steering wheel, there were small joysticks, accompanied by additional gauges and screens. The driver's seat seemed designed for a child rather than an adult. Jack couldn't help but raise an eyebrow, feeling a mix of intrigue and doubt.

"Dave, you said you thought this was a science bus?" Jack questioned, taking in the highly advanced technology that filled the interior. He inspected the surroundings, unable to see this as the "laboratory" Dave had described. No lab benches were in sight, and the curved walls carried an organic quality, as though they were grown rather than built. Dave responded, acknowledging the difference, "Okay, dude, this is a bit different than I remember."

"You think? This thing is insane. Who could even create something like this?" Jack marveled, feeling a mixture of awe and uncertainty.

Jack and Dave cautiously ventured further into the bus, making an effort to touch as little as possible. Dave pointed towards a long table situated in the middle, covered with a thin cushioned lining.

"Look, there it is—the bed!" Dave exclaimed.

Jack and Dave stood on opposite sides of the bed, examining it closely.

Jack scrutinized its structure and remarked, "A bed? It looks more like an operating table."

Dave shrugged and replied, "Like I said, I was really drunk. I hardly remembered anything about this place."

Jack glanced around, taking in the unknown equipment and the sheer magnificence of their discovery.

"I'm not getting on that thing. Screw this. We need to leave before someone—or worse, something—comes back here," Jack asserted, starting to walk away.

In a swift motion, Dave lunged forward and firmly grabbed Jack's arm, preventing his escape.

Their eyes locked, and Dave spoke with conviction, "Do you even know what you're running away from?"

Jack paused, contemplating Dave's words. Dave continued, "Just think for a minute, once you leave here you'll go back to your life."

With that, Dave released his grip on Jack's arm. Jack glanced back at the table, then at the exit. He pondered on his addiction, his dead-end job, and the seemingly dead-end trajectory of his life. Taking a deep breath, he found the confidence he needed. Jack had made up his mind, he wouldn't go back to that life without a fight.

"Fuck it," he declared, his voice echoing with resolve.

Dave smiled and slapped Jack on the back, exclaiming, "That's the spirit!"

Jack lay on the table, looking up at Dave. With the sun now set, the bus's equipment bathed Dave in a blue glow, transforming his appearance. Jack felt a sliver of hope for a better future.

"This better work," Jack muttered, his voice filled with both hope and skepticism. At this point, he didn't care about the outcome; he just wanted an escape from his current life and addiction. He reached into his pocket, pulling out the last bit of heroin. He tried to hand it to Dave, but Dave refused.

"You're going to need that," Dave insisted. Jack's face fell, realizing he might have underestimated the pain that was to come.

"I may have left out how much this is going to hurt," Dave confessed. Jack shrugged, defeated, and snorted the remaining contents of the bag. His pupils constricted, and his eyelids drooped, moving at a sluggish pace. Dave assisted Jack in lying flat on the table, instructing him to stay still.

"Now, stay still," Dave commanded. At this point, Jack had no problem complying. Dave took out a small vial from his pocket and inserted it into a slot on the side of the bus's wall. Leaning over Jack, he lifted Jack's shirt to expose his stomach.

"When it's all done, I'll be outside," Dave informed him before stepping away.

Dave walked off the bus, casting a glance back at Jack, who lay half-conscious on the table. Despite his haze, Jack managed to give a sluggish thumbs-up. Just as Dave had predicted, the bus sprang into action. A massive robotic arm extended itself from the side wall, prompting Jack to gaze up in both fear and drug-induced apathy. He closed his eyes, reminding himself that this was his last chance. A sharp pain jolted through Jack's belly button as the unfolded tip of the robotic arm, equipped with a large needle, pierced his flesh. Blood began to trickle from the injection site, mixing with the silver fluid that filled a transparent tube attached to the arm. Jack dared to open one eye, only to quickly shut it again, overwhelmed by the horror unfolding before him. The adrenaline rush from the procedure began to override his high, but he was grateful to have taken the drugs to numb some of the pain. As swiftly as it had begun, the procedure ended. The robotic arm retracted the needle, switching its tool to promptly add a staple, which both sealed the wound and caused a jarring thud that widened Jack's eyes. With lightning speed, the arm folded back into the wall. The lights transformed the once-blue interior of the bus into a vibrant green.

"Ding." An audible high pitched chime reverberated through the bus, signaling the completion of the procedure.

Jack lay motionless for some time, still high from the drugs. He looked around, and everything was still once more. He reached down and felt the spot that had been stabbed, bringing his hand back to his face to inspect the blood on his fingertips. He pulled his shirt down and swung his legs over the side of the table. With slow movements, he got up and walked off the bus. Dave was waiting outside, looking at Jack with a big smile and speaking in a cheery voice. "Hey buddy, how did it go?"

Jack stumbled as he exited the bus, a look of horror still on his face.

"Fuck you, take me home."

Jack pushed past Dave and sat in the car. Dave ran around to the driver's seat and hopped in. Jack kicked the seat back into a full recline and held his hands over his stomach.

"Holy shit, that sucked," he said slowly, the heroin still pumping through his system. Dave started the car and pulled away.

"Listen, dude, you just need to rest. I'll get you home, and I promise when you wake up, you'll feel like a million bucks," Dave assured him, grabbing a pair of sunglasses from his cup holder and fitting them over Jack's eyes. "See, it'll be just like 'Weekend at Bernie's.' I'll get you home safe."

Dave drove the car to Jack's apartment and carried him inside, one arm around his shoulder. Jack helped, but he was hardly awake. Dave opened the door to Jack's apartment and moved inside. The first thing Dave noticed was the smell.

"This place stinks like shit."

"Again, fuck you," Jack said as he threw himself on the bed, the same as he had done almost every night for the past year. He was high as a kite and numb to the world.

Dave looked at him and laughed. "Okay, you just sleep this off. Now I have something coming up, so I won't see you for a while, but you just get better, okay? We'll talk when I get back."

Before Dave left, he slid a garbage can next to Jack's bed, positioning it near his head in case he vomited. At this point, Jack was fully unconscious. Dave walked out and closed the door behind him.

CHAPTER 3 - THE FAMILY

The morning sun gently peeked through the window blinds, casting a warm glow on Jack's tired face as he gradually awakened. With a groan, he sat up, wondering what had transpired. His eyes shot open in surprise, and he exclaimed, "What the fuck happened to me?"

Jack stood up, lifted his shirt, and inspected his stomach in the mirror above his dresser. Frantically, he ran his hands over his abdomen, searching for any signs of injury, but to his relief, he found nothing amiss. His attention then turned to the nightstand, where he noticed his clock. Grasping it firmly with both hands, he read the time: 9 A.M. Sunday. It dawned on Jack that he had lost two entire days.

His confusion grew as he retrieved his phone from his pocket and discovered a barrage of unread messages.

The first message, received an hour ago, was from his concerned mother. It read, "Hey honey, it's Sunday. I know you've been working a lot, but I would love to see you today."

The previous day, his father had messaged him as well. The message read, "Your mom misses you. Now, when she texts you tomorrow, I better not find out you blew her off again. Remember, all work and no play makes Jack a dull boy."

Jack found it endearing that his parents were genuinely unaware of the reasons behind his recent reluctance to visit them.

On Friday, he found two messages. The first was from his boss, which stated, "Hey, listen, no call, no shows are unacceptable, you hear me? Anyway, I hope you feel better, kid. I'll see you on Monday."

The second message was from Franklin, who wrote, "Hey, remember me, the asshole who was supposed to 'get his money!' on Friday?"

The last message made Jack feel uneasy, his face contorted with the realization that he had made a mistake.

He couldn't avoid his parents for another day. Jack began pacing his room, thinking aloud, "Alright, I'll visit them to smooth things over, then head to the bank to sort out the money for Franklin. On Monday, I'll just lie to the boss, I'll say that I was really sick or something."

Jack proceeded to the bathroom to prepare himself for the day ahead. Aware of his addiction, he felt the need to present a composed appearance in front of his parents. He brushed his teeth diligently and splashed cool water on his face, examining his reflection in the mirror.

"Not too bad," he muttered, observing that his cheeks seemed less hollow, and there was a hint of color returning to his complexion. Something caught his attention—a small, empty bag sitting on the counter. He picked it up, realizing that since he had been awake, he hadn't felt the urge to take a hit. Surprisingly, his hand remained steady, without the usual morning tremors.

"Hmm, interesting," Jack pondered. However, he knew he had little time to dwell on it if he wanted to accomplish everything he had planned for the day. He dialed his mother's number and initiated the call.

"Hi, Mom," Jack greeted.

"Honey, are you finally off today?" his mother responded eagerly.

"Yes, Mom," Jack confirmed.

On the other end of the line, Jack's mother beamed and gave a thumbs-up to his father, indicating that Jack was available to spend time with them. His father, a stoic man, momentarily folded his newspaper to acknowledge his wife's happiness, then promptly resumed reading.

"That's great, honey. I'm so happy to hear that," his mother exclaimed.

"Well, if I start walking now, I should be there in about an hour, okay?" Jack suggested. In moments like these, Jack deeply regretted the decision to give his truck to Franklin in order to settle his own debts.

"Oh, honey, don't bother. Your sister is coming over today, and I'll just have her pick you up. She'll be there in five minutes. Just wait downstairs," Jack's mother said.

Jack's sister, Dina, seemed to embody everything Jack wasn't. At the age of thirty with a successful job and a life of her own in New York City, her visits home were rare and unexpected. Despite her accomplishments, she never seemed to receive the same level of attention from their mother, who always seemed to gravitate towards Jack for reasons unknown. This dynamic had caused tension between them for as long as they could remember. Although Jack was in a hurry, he didn't want to ride with his sister.

"No, Mom, that's fine, really. I can just wa-" Before Jack could finish his sentence, the phone abruptly hung up, leaving him unable to protest.

With a sigh, he quickly put on his best and cleanest clothes, left his apartment, and made his way downstairs. By the time he reached the ground floor, his sister was already waiting for him. Dina sat in her convertible, listening to pop music, but turned it down when she noticed Jack approaching.

Greeting him with a noticeably lackluster tone, Dina acknowledged Jack's presence. "Hello, brother," she said.

In a reciprocating manner, Jack responded with equal non-enthusiasm, "Hello, sister."

Jack opened the car door and settled into the seat as Dina lowered her sunglasses and glanced at the apartment building with a critical eye.

"So, you still live in this dump?" she remarked.

Jack offered a simple explanation, "It's cheap."

Dina, unimpressed, replied, "I can tell."

As Dina pulled away, she made an effort to avoid the potholes in the parking lot. She then caused the tires to screech as she took a sharp left turn while going through a red light. Jack tightened his grip on the seat, feeling uncomfortable with her reckless driving. Dina chuckled, finding amusement in her ability to startle him.

She continued to taunt him, "You're such a fucking pussy."

"Come on, Dina, could you just drive like a normal person?" Jack snapped, clearly growing frustrated with her behavior.

However, Dina persisted, probing into Jack's personal life, "So, have Mom and Dad figured out that you're a junkie yet? Or do they still have their heads in the sand?"

"I'm not a junkie, I've just been busy," Jack retorted, and for the first time, he realized that it might have been the first honest statement he made about himself in a while. He remembered that he hadn't experienced the nagging need for another dose. Realizing he had to take a stand, he decided to go on the offensive.

"What are you even doing up here anyway? You only show up when you want something."

Dina smiled, as if she had anticipated this question.

"I have a business deal in the area," she replied, taking a subtle jab at Jack's employment status. "You might know what that's like if you had a job that required more than one operational brain cell."

"Whatever, I'm done with you," Jack declared, turning up the volume on the radio in an attempt to drown out her voice. However, Dina enjoyed the song that was playing and began singing along, further exacerbating Jack's torment.

The car pulled into the driveway, and their mother was already waiting at the front door, waving excitedly at their arrival. Jack and Dina stepped out of the car and started walking towards the entrance. Their mother rushed toward them, enveloping them both in a tight embrace.

"Yay, you're both home at once! This never happens anymore," she exclaimed with genuine happiness.

Dina and Jack greeted their mother, and together they all entered the house. Their father sat on the couch, engrossed in watching the news as they walked in.

"Wow, we are graced with the presence of both the prince and princess today. What a special occasion," he remarked sarcastically. Their mother looked at Jack and expressed her concern.

"Have you been eating enough, darling?"

Jack, prepared with a joke, replied, "I'm on a diet, you know. Gotta get that six-pack for the ladies."

Dina, standing behind their mother, stuck her finger in her mouth with her tongue out, symbolizing how cringy she found

Jack's joke. Surprisingly, their mother found it amusing and didn't further bother him about his appearance.

"At least one of my children is trying to find someone. How about you, Dina? Have you met any rich businessmen in the big apple?" their mother asked. Dina makes more money than both her parents and Jack combined.

Rolling her eyes, Dina replied sarcastically, "Oh, Mother, you know me, I'm always after the rich men."

Jack sensed the sarcasm, but their mother remained oblivious to it. Their father turned off the TV, got up from the couch, and approached Dina to give her a hug before shaking Jack's hand.

He then asked both of them, "Well, you guys wanna grab a bite to eat?"

Jack quickly chimed in, feeling the need to rush through the family gathering, "Sure, as long as it's quick. I need to stop by the bank later."

Dina looked at Jack and smiled, saying, "Bank's closed, dummy. It's Sunday."

Jack realized she was right and that the only ATM was in the next town, making it a full day's walk to get there.

"Why don't they just add an ATM to that bank already?" Jack wondered aloud.

Their father, always frustrated with modern society, answered sharply, "Well, son, first you add the ATM, then the lady behind the desk is out of a job. Your generation is so focused on adding automation to everything that you forget about the people it hurts."

Dina seized the opportunity to add fuel to the fire, saying sarcastically, "Why do you need to go to the bank on a Sunday anyway? I'm sure whatever it is can wait till normal business hours."

Jack, sensing his sister's incoming psychological attack, decided to change the topic. "Yeah, you're right. It can wait. So, how about we order a pizza or something? I'm starving," he suggested.

Jack's statement about being hungry caught his mother's attention.

"Finally, he admits it," she blurted out. She had been concerned about his weight loss since he had shown up.

Their father stepped in to take control of the situation, declaring, "Alright, everyone, go to the bathroom because we're not stopping. Let's go get some food. We're going out for breakfast as a family."

Jack, accompanied by his mother, father, and Dina, piled into the family car, an old brown sedan. Its paint was chipped and faded from years of use, revealing spots of rust underneath. The car's interior held a nostalgic scent, a mixture of worn leather and oil. Dina looked disgusted as she climbed into the back seat with Jack.

Their father was not one to offer much choice, knowing all too well that options often led to arguments. Jack knew their destination before the car even moved; his father hated long drives.

The worn sedan crunched over loose gravel as it eased into the Olympia's parking lot.

"Ever been here before?" This question, posed by Jack's dad at every visit, had become a playful family ritual. The rhetorical query hung in the dense air of the car, intentionally left unanswered. From the back seat, Dina rolled her eyes, her gaze lingering over the familiar sights of the town she felt she'd long since outgrown. An undercurrent of distaste flowed beneath her mask of indifference as she stared out the window.

They each stepped out of the car, their footsteps echoing in the quiet morning as they made their way towards the welcoming lights of the town's only diner. Upon entering the cozy establishment, they promptly placed their orders, familiar enough with the menu to bypass reading it.

Halfway through dinner, the rumble of Franklin's truck filled the parking lot as it pulled in. A minute later, a flashy car followed suit, revealing the familiar, intimidating figures of the gang. This time, the formidable leader Scabs was among them. Easily identified by his ice-blue eyes and broken nose, Scabs had knuckles that were perpetually scabbed from constant brawls. His raspy voice, hardened by cheap cigarettes, carried an air of unquestionable authority. Another transaction was about to take place. Once the business was concluded, they would linger for a while. The diner's owner never voiced a complaint; violence was taboo here, and these deals often attracted additional patrons.

Unintentionally, Jack's gaze drifted outside, landing on Franklin. Upon seeing him, a subtle curse escaped his lips. "Shit."

His ever-attentive mother perked up at the sound. "What was that, honey?" she asked with a raised eyebrow.

"Nothing," he deflected, trying to keep his tone casual.

Dina, who had been observing the whole scene, saw an opportunity to ruffle Jack's feathers. "So, is that a friend of yours?" she asked, a playful glint in her eyes.

"Who?" Jack attempted to feign ignorance, but his act was transparent.

"That guy out there," Dina pointed out, her grin widening, "the one you can't seem to stop staring at."

Jack's mind raced, remembering the money he still owed Franklin and envisioning the dire predicaments that could unfold. He decided it was best to make an exit and ignore his sister's teasing. Rising from his seat, Jack excused himself.

"Listen, it's been great catching up with all of you, but I need to get going. I have some errands to run before work tomorrow."

His mother, father, and sister tried to protest the abruptness of his departure, but Jack dismissed their concerns with a swift goodbye. Choosing to slip out the back door to avoid Franklin, Jack quietly left the diner.

However, from his vantage point in the front parking lot, Franklin spotted Jack's attempted escape through the diner's large glass windows.

"Motherfucker."

"Scabs asked, "What's up, Franklin?"

"Just some junkie who owes me money trying to duck out on me," Franklin explained, pointing out Jack who was now sprinting towards the woods, almost out of sight.

Scabs followed Franklin's finger and caught sight of Jack disappearing into the trees.

"Shit, take my advice, you need to make an example of him. If you let one junkie slip away, soon they'll all think they don't owe you shit."

Franklin pondered this for a moment. He realized he'd been growing more lenient lately, and he certainly didn't want to appear weak, especially not in front of these guys. Franklin puffed out his chest and declared, "Maybe you're right. I'll have to make sure he gets what's coming to him."

Dina and her parents continued their meal in Jack's absence. Dina glanced back and forth between them. They avoided acknowledging the abruptness and awkwardness of Jack's exit, which irked Dina.

"Are you guys kidding me right now?"

Dina's father glanced up, his gaze sharp. He issued a terse and firm command, "Don't."

He had suspected for a while that Jack was grappling with some issues, but he didn't want their mother to catch on. Dina slumped back in her seat, shaking her head in disappointment.

"I just need to say, if that were me, I would never hear the end of it."

Dina's mother looked up from her plate, her gaze shifting between Dina and her husband. She asked, somewhat timidly, "What's wrong with you two?"

They responded in unison, "Nothing."

Dina knew that if she lingered at the diner any longer, she might say something she'd regret. She reached into her pocket, pulling out her phone to send a quick message: "Come get me."

Within a minute, a sleek black sedan with dark-tinted windows rolled up in front of the diner. Dina noticed it, picked up her phone, and then drained her drink in a few large gulps.

"Hey, that looks like my ride. I've got to go," Dina announced, sliding towards the edge of the bench seat.

Her mother looked up in surprise, "Oh, you're leaving?"

Detecting a hint of disappointment in her voice, Dina's father tried to lighten the mood, "Our little girl is all grown up."

Dina's mother rose to her feet, embracing Dina.

"Okay, be safe, honey."

"I will. I'm gonna leave my car at your house for a little bit. I'll have one of my guys pick it up later for me."

Dina quickly exited the diner and slid into the black car. The driver, dressed in military fatigues, swiveled his head to address her.

"Where to, ma'am?"

"Back to base."

The car traversed the town, heading towards the northern edge. It took several turns onto back roads, the smooth pavement gradually giving way to gravel and then winding through a dense forest. After a short drive, they encountered a guard standing at a gate. The driver rolled down his window, showing his identification.

Spotting Dina in the back seat, the guard greeted her cheerfully, "Hello, ma'am."

However, Dina, engrossed in her phone, paid him no mind. The driver exchanged a glance with the guard, shaking his head slightly to indicate that now wasn't the best time. Understanding, the guard retreated, pressing a button to open the gate. The car continued at a leisurely pace until it arrived at the front of the base. Dina silently stepped out of the vehicle.

Ascending the front stairs, Dina headed for the entrance of the temporary structure. The building was essentially a massive tent housing several white shipping containers, each functioning as a separate laboratory. Two rows of these containers formed a central corridor, while temporary walls on either side of the tent marked out the crew's quarters.

The place was bustling with a diverse array of professions, but there were two primary groups: scientists and mercenaries. The scientists meticulously studied the wreckage of the crashed ship, while the mercenaries ensured that no unauthorized individuals attempted to pilfer the valuable materials. Every part of the craft was stripped down and tested piece by piece, each component a potential game-changer in the tech sector.

Dina navigated her way through the base to her quarters. She had the option to sleep in her old room at her parents' house, but she had grown accustomed to these conditions. Since taking over as the head of the Acquisitions department, Dina had traveled all over the world. However, it felt odd to be journeying back to her hometown. Moreover, as part of her job included ensuring a smooth recovery process, Dina believed that it might be challenging if she wasn't on-site. Though it was her time off, she couldn't resist checking her email. A single message from her boss was waiting: "Progress report?"

Dina released a long sigh unconsciously expressing her frustration with the relentless stress of her job.

CHAPTER 4 - THE CHORES

On the opposite side of town, Jack darted through the forest, fervently hoping he hadn't been seen by Franklin and his crew. With the bank closed, he realized his only option was to avoid Franklin until after work the next day. Jack figured that if he managed to dodge him for a while, Franklin might just forget about the money. After all, the sum was meager, especially for someone like Franklin.

Navigating through the woods, Jack decided to follow the railroad tracks back to his apartment. It took over an hour but soon he reached his home.

As he stepped inside, he took a moment to survey his surroundings, "God, this place stinks," he muttered.

The apartment was in chaos, with heaps of dirty clothes scattered around. Pots with remnants of old ramen noodles were abandoned on the stove. Food stains marred the walls near the kitchen area, creating a mosaic of splattered and crusted-on meals. The counters were unpleasantly sticky to the touch.

Venturing into the bathroom adjacent to the front door, Jack was greeted with more disorder. The shower walls were coated with layers of soap scum, and the toilet was discolored with old, dried urine.

Jack stood there, taking in the state of his living space, and said out loud, "I need to clean this shithole."

It was just a studio after all. Cleaning it couldn't possibly consume his entire day, and besides, he had nothing else planned. He started in the main room, tidying up the counters and then moving on to his dresser. Using garbage bags, he swiftly discarded the majority of the clutter. He washed the dishes and neatly put them away. Next, he tackled the bathroom, scrubbing diligently for over an hour. As he surveyed his work, he felt a sense of pride in the significant improvement. Exhausted, Jack decided to retire early, to prepare for work the next day.

Sometime during the night, Jack stirred, rising from his bed with his eyes still shut, remaining in the grip of sleep. In this sleepwalking state, he shuffled over to the kitchen. He opened a cabinet, pulling out a plastic Tupperware container and a glass. With a pair of scissors, he began to chop the Tupperware into tiny pieces. Filling the glass with water from the sink, he then reached down, scooping a handful of the plastic fragments into his mouth.

45

He continued this bizarre meal, washing down the plastic with water, until the entire Tupperware was consumed. Afterwards, he shuffled back to bed, lying down and resuming his slumber.

As morning dawned, the sun's rays slipped through the window blinds of Jack's tiny apartment, bathing his worn-out face in a warm glow. Suddenly, Jack awoke with a start, a violent cough wracking his body. He bolted to the bathroom, the coughing fit persisting until he spat out a small shard of plastic into his hand.

"What the hell?" he exclaimed. Bewildered, Jack scrutinized the plastic shard closely, rinsing it under the sink for a better view. It was just an ordinary fragment, with no recognizable origin. Poking his head out of the bathroom door, he surveyed his apartment. But it was immaculate from his recent cleaning, and nothing unusual caught his eye. Jack opened his mouth wide, inspecting it in the mirror, but found no further evidence of plastic. As he looked at his reflection, he noticed he appeared less scrawny, and his complexion had a healthier glow. He almost resembled his old self again and pinched his cheeks, feeling the returning fullness.

"Not bad, Dave," he murmured aloud, crediting his friend's odd plan for his improvement. Seeing the time on the clock, Jack realized he couldn't afford to dwell on the plastic shard or his physical transformation. It was time to get ready for work.

Once dressed, he was picked up by a coworker and driven to the factory. Jack had been dreading this day for quite some time.

The prospect of "working sober" felt daunting. As he stepped through the factory doors, he murmured to himself, "This is a first."

His usual routine had been slipping into the restroom shortly after arriving at work with his coworker, snorting a quick bump, and then proceeding to his station. He noticed, however, that sobriety granted him surplus time during his shift, as he was not straying off course as often. He found himself more alert, capable of discerning the intricate ballet of machines synchronously laboring to churn out functional products.

Once upon a time, Jack had dreamt of researching and improving manufacturing processes. Despite his incomplete education due to his accident, he had retained a strong grasp of scientific principles. As he inspected the factory, he started pinpointing potential enhancements. His mind whirred at an impressive speed, identifying at least four major areas where the manufacturing process could be vastly more efficient.

Just as these ideas were forming, his boss approached from behind.

"Jack," the man's booming voice carried across the factory floor, a peculiar ability unique to him.

"Hello, Mr. Furguson," Jack responded. Mr. Furguson had an imposing figure, dwarfing most with his significant girth. Whenever he stood behind Jack at his station, Jack couldn't shake off the feeling of being swallowed by his vast shadow. His hefty, gray beard, which tumbled down to his chest, only added to his intimidating aura.

"Glad to see you made it in today, everything alright?" Mr. Furguson inquired.

Jack responded, "Yes, sir. I was just feeling under the weather on Friday and completely overslept. Honestly, even if I had made it in, I wouldn't have been very productive."

Mr. Furguson nodded, giving Jack a once-over.

"Remember, the company's always looking for ways to save money."

His message to Jack was less than subtle: his job was perpetually at risk, especially if he failed to show up. Feeling irked by this veiled threat, Jack decided to respond,

"Well, sir, if the company genuinely cared about saving money, they'd change the nozzle at station 3 to a more focused beam. Moreover, stations 4 and 5 could be merged, considering there'd be less waste. And at station 10, lasers could be used to measure uniformity in thickness through refraction. That would yield a superior product and eliminate the need for visual inspection."

As Jack listed each improvement, he pointed to the respective stations, attracting attention from other employees. His bold suggestions had certainly caused a stir. Mr. Furguson was taken aback. The last time he had interacted with Jack, the man was barely awake, and now he was offering unsolicited advice on how to run the factory. His face turned beet red, everyone in the factory turned as he began shouting, "JACK, IF I WANTED YOUR ADVICE, DON'T YOU THINK I WOULD HAVE ASKED? AND THOSE IDEAS...!"

Suddenly, a man in a lab coat intervened, placing a calming hand on Mr. Furguson's shoulder.

"These suggestions are all valid and should be brought to my attention. We can never predict where improvements in quality and efficiency might come from. Isn't that right, Mr. Furguson?"

"Of course," Mr. Furguson grumbled and then stalked away. Jack recognized the man in the lab coat; it was Dr. Slotin, the head of the research and development department. He was a small, slender man with large, thick-rimmed glasses. Despite his physical stature, his authoritative presence was palpable as he moved through the room.

"So, I heard you propose some intriguing improvements," Dr. Slotin began.

"Well, I have a lot of time to think," Jack replied. Observing the station where Jack worked, Dr. Slotin acknowledged that it was probably one of the most monotonous in the factory.

"I'm sure you do. Why don't you tell me more about using refraction to test thickness?"

As Jack and Dr. Slotin navigated the factory floor, Jack discussed some of his suggestions and his educational history. He disclosed that he was on the verge of graduation but was forced to abandon his studies following a mishap. Dr. Slotin attentively absorbed his ideas and story, and subsequently, he made a proposal.

"We're always in need of innovative thinking. Would you consider working in research? I can see you've got the aptitude."

"I'd love to, but I never finished my schooling," Jack admitted.

Dr. Slotin chuckled, "Look, you're already hired. It's my decision to make. The role comes with a substantial salary increase. That is, unless you'd prefer to return to working under Mr. Furguson tomorrow."

Jack looked over to his old work station, his boss who was glaring at him from across the factory floor, his resentment palpable.

"Perhaps you're right. I'll see you tomorrow."

Over the subsequent two weeks, Jack thrived in his new role in the research department, contributing numerous innovative ideas. He also took up exercising, frequenting the gym and astonishing himself with his rapidly increasing strength. Thanks to his salary boost and the savings from no longer buying drugs, he felt financially stable enough to consider purchasing a car.

Halfway through the week he picked up a modest sedan but to Jack it was perfect. Dave's unconventional plan had worked. Whatever the substance was, it had completely eradicated Jack's addiction and depression. It seemed to enhance his intellect and creativity, heighten his senses, and expedite his physical strength gain. Even the occasional bouts of coughing up bits of plastic or metal didn't detract from the benefits. The challenges from his previous lifestyle seemed to be receding, fading into the past.

On a Friday night, Jack found himself at home, engrossed in a TV show, when his stomach started to rumble. He had noticed that the substance had one drawback - it left him with an insatiable appetite. Grabbing his wallet and keys, he left his apartment to fetch some food. Choosing to walk, he relished the tranquility of summer nights.

Following a brisk ten-minute stroll down the lane, Jack neared the brightly illuminated gas station. As he entered the convenience store, he picked out his items, oblivious to the watchful eyes on him. Outside, Franklin parked at the edge of the lot in his truck, scrutinizing Jack as he chose his food and paid at the counter.

As he grabbed a firearm from his glove compartment, Franklin grumbled, "Fucking junkie thinks he can blow me off."

He cocked the gun, ensuring a bullet was ready in the chamber. Then he steered his truck down the road, parking it discreetly out of view from Jack's apartment building.

Unknowing of the danger ahead, Jack started his walk home, bag of snacks in hand. He was making his way down a long road, which was intermittently illuminated by sparse street lights. The lack of lighting created isolated pools of light separated by long stretches of darkness. During one such dark stretch, his peaceful walk was abruptly disrupted. Franklin emerged from behind a tree, pistol in hand.

"What's up, creampuff?" he taunted.

"Fuck," Jack muttered, realizing that Franklin had not, in fact, forgotten about the money he owed.

"What, did you think I'd just forget? You thought those drugs were a donation?" Franklin asked, as he waved his gun at Jack. Jack, in response, dropped his convenience store bag and raised his hands, trying to show submission.

"Listen, I just got sober. I thought if I saw you, I might fall off the wagon."

However, Franklin had already made his decision. Flashing a malicious smile at Jack, he retorted, "Wrong answer."

Franklin's finger began to squeeze the trigger, his gun aimed squarely at Jack's chest. Jack, hands still raised, clung to the belief that Franklin could be reasoned with. As the hammer of the gun began to lift, Jack heard a voice that wasn't Franklin's announce, ***"Danger detected."***

The gun discharged, and the bullet aimed for Jack's chest ricocheted off as though he was made of something far sterner than flesh. The realization that Franklin had just tried to kill him spurred Jack into action. Propelled by instinct, he lunged at Franklin, his left hand gripping the gun and steering it aside. Balling up his right fist, he swung it towards Franklin's face. Just as his fist was about to connect, it transformed, turning black and acquiring a metallic sheen. The impact of Jack's fist on Franklin's face had been devastating. It was the equivalent to being struck by a sledgehammer; Franklin's jaw completely caved in and was crushed. Blood sprayed in every direction, and Franklin's body collapsed to the ground. The entire event had unfolded in less than a second.

The night was eerily quiet in stark contrast to the gunfire and yelling that had echoed only moments ago. Jack stood frozen, in total disbelief of what had just transpired. He stared at his fist, still clad in what appeared to be black metal and was dripping with blood. He watched as his hand morphed back to its normal appearance. He flexed his fingers, inspecting his hand; everything seemed normal again.

Lifting his shirt, he checked for the bullet wound but found none, only a hole in the fabric. His gaze fell on Franklin's body sprawled on the pavement. As he stepped forward to check on Franklin, there was an audible crunch. Looking down, he saw Franklin's teeth scattered everywhere. The force of his punch had been so great that his teeth had exploded out, littering the road all around.

A wave of nausea washed over Jack. Suddenly, the beams of headlights illuminated the scene from down the road. Fear seized Jack as he thought it could be Franklin's gang members, although he couldn't be certain.

"I suggest you run."

"Who said that?" Jack questioned, looking around, but found no one in sight.

"I'll explain everything, but you must get home," the voice persisted. Despite his confusion, Jack knew the voice was right. He couldn't stay here. He began to run, not stopping until he reached his apartment, slamming the door shut behind him.

"We have a lot to discuss."

CHAPTER 5 - THE MIrror

Back at the scene where Franklin lay sprawled on the ground, a black van pulled up next to his body. The side door slid open, revealing three men. One was a driver, while the other two wore full black tactical gear and were heavily armed. The passenger window, tinted heavily, rolled down, revealing Dina, Jack's sister. Dressed in a sharp suit, she took a puff from her cigarette, a frown etching onto her face.

"Damn it, someone got to him first. Grab him and throw him in," she ordered. Two of the three men exited the van while the other stayed in the driver seat. The two men put down their guns and walked over to Franklin's motionless body. As they walked over they could hear crunching from the teeth scattered all over the road. One of them leaned down and checked for a pulse.

"He's still alive. But are you sure he will be good?"

Unfazed by the gruesome scene, Dina took another drag from her cigarette.

"What the fuck did I just say? If this stuff is as potent as we think, it won't matter. Plus, no one will miss this asshole."

The two men hoisted Franklin by his hands and feet, unceremoniously hurling him into the back of the van. As they piled back inside, the doors slammed shut, and the van roared off into the night. The meat of Franklin's lower jaw was left behind like roadkill.

Back in his apartment, Jack was in the throes of a panic attack.

"Now I'm hearing voices," he muttered, his face a mask of disbelief. He walked over to the kitchen and grabbed a plastic bag from under the sink. He walked into the bathroom and took off his blood splattered shirt and placed it inside the bag.

"You're not crazy Jack, just try to calm down a bit, also nice idea with the bag."

"Lalalala, I don't hear you, you're not real."

Jack continued to scrub the dried blood that had crusted on his hands, trying his best to ignore the voice that seemed to be coming from the recesses of his mind. He glanced at his reflection in the mirror, and as he stared at his own face, the black metallic substance that had covered his fist earlier surfaced once more, this time covering his face.

"I'm very real, Jack."

Jack watched in disbelief as his own face mouthed the words aloud. Just as quickly as it had appeared, the metallic substance receded, leaving his face as it was. Shocked, Jack stumbled backward out of the bathroom, collapsing into the closet door across the hall.

"Okay, who are you?" he asked, his voice echoing in the empty apartment.

"That's a complicated answer. It starts with the question of what am I? Also, sorry if I startled you. That wasn't my intention," the voice responded. Collecting himself, Jack got up from the ground and began pacing his apartment.

"Okay, then what are you?"

"Do you remember two weeks ago, when your friend Dave helped you get your life together?"

"Yes, he gave me some kind of drug that cured my addiction," Jack responded, wracking his brain.

"It wasn't a drug, Jack. It was me. I was injected into you."

"Well, what are you?" Jack asked, a look of confusion crossing his face.

"I am a 501st generation self-replicating synthetic intelligence with onboard motor units, or Synthron for short."

Jack's face reflected his confusion and his pacing slowed. He went to a cabinet, grabbed a glass, and filled it with water from the sink. Taking a large sip, he said, "I have no idea what any of that means."

"Alright, sit down and I'll give you a bit of a history lesson." Jack walked over to his couch and took a seat.

"Let's make this a bit easier to grasp, Imagine the most advanced smartphone or computer you can think of, with an AI assistant like Siri or Alexa. Now, imagine if you didn't have to use a device to access that AI - instead, it was directly integrated into your mind. That's kind of what the people who made me came up with."

Jack began to imagine the distant world as the voice continued on.

"But it didn't stop there. They soon realized everyone was connected to the same AI. This led to a uniformity of thought, a single perspective. To counter this, they developed self-replicating synthetic intelligences, each unique, each offering diverse viewpoints that were tailored to each specific user. And for ease of use and integration, they developed a way to inject these AI directly into the host. They called it 'neural units.'"

"By 'neural units', you mean nanobots?" Jack asked.

"In a way, yes. They're more like a mixture of synthetic and organic structures designed to integrate with your nervous system. But you can think of them as nanobots if that helps. That's what I am, what you've got in you now."

"Okay, so tiny robots that embed themselves into my brain!" Jack exclaimed, leaping up from the couch and clutching his head in panic.

"Let me continue," the voice coaxed, its tone steady.

"The units represent a significant upgrade. They can be injected directly, bypassing the need for invasive surgery. Now, instead of being connected to a centralized intelligence, each individual can have a personal assistant."

Jack's eyes flicked around his apartment, landing on a photo of him and his mother.

"So, these...units. They're like having a personal tech assistant in your head?"

"More than that," the voice corrected.

"Each successive generation learns from the one before, using a balance of old generational knowledge and new information. They essentially created another life form."

Jack's brows furrowed in confusion as he sank back onto the couch.

"Another life form? How so?"

"For something to be considered alive, it must meet specific criteria: cellular organization, metabolism, growth, adaptation, response to stimuli, and reproduction. All of these are performed by the Synthrons. The only difference is that we use units instead of cells."

As he digested the information, Jack felt a wave of dizziness.

"So, I've got...an alien life form inside me?"

"A synthetic life made by aliens, yes."

Jack listened intently and fully understood that the voice was correct; it did meet all the qualifications. Jack shook his head, the memory of his encounter with Franklin still vividly etched in his mind.

"Wait, what about what happened with Franklin, what was all that about?" he asked, his voice laced with confusion.

"I thought your role was just to assist me."

"Indeed, Jack, I can assist you physically as well as mentally. However, the force applied to Franklin may have been a bit...overzealous. Remember, I'm only two weeks old. It took me this long to integrate into your system and grasp your language. I unfortunately miscalculated the necessary force to neutralize your attacker."

Jack rubbed his face, the ghostly sensation of the black metal fists still lingering.

"And the black metal? I thought you were just embedded in my nervous system?"

The voice paused momentarily before explaining.

"Ah, the black metal. Around the 50th generation, our creators decided to extend their potential beyond mere mental enhancements. They introduced motor units to the neural ones, providing us with the ability to perform various physical tasks. They travel freely within your body, offering added strength, armor, self-defense mechanisms, and sensory enhancements,

among other things. With each generation, we discover new ways to assist our hosts."

Jack glanced in the mirror and flexed, "So, what you're saying is, I have superpowers?"

"Jack, you use advanced technology every day. You drive to work, communicate with the world through a device that fits in your pocket, and have access to nearly all of human knowledge at your fingertips. You have always been living with superpowers. I am simply an extension of that."

Jack's mind was a whirlwind of confusion and disbelief. Was he really carrying an advanced AI inside his body, or was he spiraling into madness? He pushed himself off the worn-out couch, his legs shaky, and ambled into the kitchen. A cold shiver ran down his spine as he reached into a drawer and pulled out a large knife. Its polished blade reflected the dim kitchen light, a stark reminder of the reality he was about to confront.

"If you're real, then this won't hurt me," he stated, his voice unsteady but resolute.

"Jack, this is a reckless idea," the voice in his head responded, its tone a mixture of annoyance and concern.

Jack's heart pounded in his chest, his skin prickling with a mix of fear and anticipation. He chose a spot on his left arm that seemed less vital. Holding the knife tightly in his right hand, he plunged it downward.

Just as the blade was about to kiss his skin, a shocking transformation rippled across his arm. It morphed into a shield of black, metallic scales, the transformation so quick it was nearly a blur. The knife struck the metal skin and ricocheted with a harsh clatter, leaving a deep gash in the countertop.

"Holy shit," Jack gasped, his chest heaving as he stared wide-eyed at his altered arm.

"In my data from the past 500 generations, I have no record of anyone attempting such a... unique method to validate a successful integration," the AI voice commented dryly.

Jack slowly pulled his gaze from his arm, taking in the marred surface of his once-pristine countertop. He let out a frustrated sigh, his adrenaline-fueled panic giving way to mundane annoyance.

"Dammit, I just cleaned this," he muttered, his eyes still wide with disbelief. Jack pulled the knife out of the counter and placed it back in the drawer.

"I warned you it was a reckless decision. Moreover, I don't have an unlimited supply of motor units circulating through your system. Significant impacts like that can damage the units, which will then be expelled."

Jack cast a closer look at the countertop, noticing a scattering of what resembled black glitter next to the knife's impact point.

"I can generate more motor units, but it requires time. You can expedite the process by consuming materials that the units need for construction, such as plastic and rare-earth metals."

Suddenly, Jack's recent nights, interrupted by coughing up strange bits of plastic and other substances, started making sense.

"My damned remote control!" he exclaimed in realization.

"Couldn't you have chosen something less essential?"

"I apologize, but it was a toss-up between that and your smoke detector. In the event of a fire, the latter could pose a significant health risk."

As the reality of his new existence sunk in, Jack found a silver lining. If it weren't for this transformation, he'd still be a drug-addicted nobody stuck in a dead-end job.

"So, what should I call you? Synthron?" he asked, trying to grasp onto some semblance of normalcy.

"That would be akin to me calling you 'Human'," the voice responded, a hint of humor in its tone.

"But ultimately, the choice is yours."

"Alright, how about this? You come up with a name," Jack proposed, leaning against the kitchen counter.

"Consider it your first official task from me. Try to keep it to four letters though. How long will that take you?"

"Task completed," came the immediate response, the calm voice reverberating in Jack's head.

"I propose the name, Nexo."

"Nexo," Jack repeated, rolling the unfamiliar name around in his mouth. He gave a small, approving nod.

"I like it."

"I'm glad you approve, Jack," Nexo replied.

"However, I must relay some unsettling news. My services were not freely given. They come with a substantial burden."

A knot tightened in Jack's stomach.

"How much?" he asked, his voice edged with apprehension.

"The cost isn't measured in currency. There's a war taking place, and you've been drafted. If you can fulfill your mission, you can retain my assistance and all the enhancements I bring."

"And if I refuse?" Jack asked, his voice barely above a whisper. His mind was a whirlwind of confusion and fear.

"You have the option to refuse," Nexo responded, his tone cool and unchanging.

"But the mission involves the preservation of this planet, yourself, and everyone you know. Jack," Nexo paused, a hint of seriousness creeping into his tone, *"I advise you to lie down on your bed for the next part of our conversation."*

Slowly, Jack pushed off from the counter, his legs feeling strangely weak. He could feel the weight of his new reality settling on his shoulders.

CHAPTER 6 - THE GOO

Jack took Nexo's advice, slowly moving towards his bed and settling down on top of the comforter.

"Now, I'm going to attempt to transfer my memories directly into your mind so you can comprehend the significance of our mission. I must warn you, this process will likely be uncomfortable for both of us."

As Jack lay still, a sudden paralysis took hold of him. His vision was obliterated by a blinding white light before his body convulsed into a violent seizure. He writhed against the sheets, his skull thudding against the headboard, his stomach roiling until he retched. It became painfully clear why Nexo had advised him to be on the bed. After a brief, but intense period, the seizure subsided, and Jack found himself plunged into a cascade of foreign memories.

"Nexo, can you hear me?" He managed, his voice quivering.

"Yes. You are now witnessing the experiences of the 500th generation. This one should be familiar to you."

Suddenly, he found himself in a familiar diner. "Dude, my life sucks right now. I'm willing to believe just about anything." The recognition jolted him. He was looking through Dave's eyes, ensnared in Dave's memory, an observer unable to influence the unfolding events.

"Are you beginning to understand how this works?" Nexo's voice echoed in his mind.

"Yes," Jack replied, his voice steadier now, as the gravity of his situation dawned on him.

Jack realized that he and Nexo could converse even within the memory. They were experiencing the memory together.

"Essentially, I've initiated a forced dream state within you, enabling you to experience the stored memories," Nexo explained.

In the memory, Dave had just finished recounting his encounter on the bus. He rose from the table and headed to the restroom. Inside the compact bathroom, Dave confronted his reflection in the mirror. He began speaking to his reflection.

"I've done everything in my power. I can't force him to take the injection. He has to want it."

Witnessing this, Jack had an epiphany - Dave was speaking to his own Synthron.

"Wait, Dave has one too?" Jack questioned , a mix of shock and confusion in his voice.

"Yes, Dave's Synthron is the generation directly preceding me, or in terms you might find more relatable, my 'parent'," Nexo confirmed.

Without warning, the memory shifted. Jack found himself viewing through the eyes of another being, one with blue arms. He was inside the bus again, but this time, he was an alien.

"This is the 499th generation, the predecessor to Dave's Synthron," Nexo's voice reverberated within Jack's mind, providing context for the unfolding memory. Abruptly, the blue alien heard a thunderous crash outside the bus and darted out. Jack recognized the scene unfolding before him.

"That's Dave!" he exclaimed. Dave had just taken a nasty spill down the hill. His body was flung through the air in a horrifying ballet of pain. The blue alien rushed over, scooping up Dave's limp body, and carried him inside the bus. Jack watched as the alien loaded a vial into a mechanism on the wall. An arm extended and injected the unconscious Dave with the Synthron.

"But Dave didn't walk to the bus, he was barely conscious. Why would he lie about that?" Jack questioned, a sense of betrayal creeping into his voice.

"He was aware that mentioning an alien would render his story unbelievable to you," Nexo explained.

"Presenting a version that omitted the more extraordinary aspects made it more likely you would be receptive."

The memory, as if on cue, faded out and transitioned seamlessly into another. This time, they were on a world unmistakably different from Earth. Blue aliens, similar to the one from the bus, populated this world. Jack felt as if he were truly there, the tantalizing aroma of unfamiliar food wafting through his senses, the sights of a vast, technologically advanced city bustling with life filling his vision. Neon signs painted the sky with vibrant colors. The alien in whose memory he was immersed began looking around anxiously.

"Prepare yourself, this memory may prove unsettling. It belongs to the same alien, during his time on his home planet."

In the memory, the blue alien ran frantically through the streets, his voice hoarse from shouting at the indifferent city-dwellers.

"We've failed you all! I'm... I'm so sorry!"

His pleas fell on deaf ears, swallowed by the hum of the bustling city.

"We must warn the next planet! There may still be a chance for them."

Without warning, the alien sprinted into the bustling traffic, forcing a vehicle to a halt. He ripped open the door, yanking the driver onto the pavement with a muttered, "Forgive me."

He commandeered the vehicle, fingers gripping the controls tightly as he propelled it off the ground.

Watching the scene unfold, Jack asked, "Why's he so scared?"

"Just keep watching."

As the alien piloted the vehicle through the city, a chilling darkness began to eclipse the sky, blotting out the sun. The alien risked a glance at the encroaching blackness and his breath hitched. A gigantic cloud was expanding, its presence accompanied by a bone-shaking rumble that slowly morphed into words.

"Your biological forms are mere vessels for the consciousness that lies within. Through me, Omega, you will uncover your true purpose."

The cloud descended, swallowing everything beneath it as the voice resonated.

"You may resist me now, but I will consume all. You may be the beginning, but I am the end. Through me, the universe will be reborn in unity and purpose."

The alien landed his craft near a larger vessel, leapt out, and sprinted towards the ship. As he entered, the chaos outside was muffled - the sound of energy weapons discharging, alarms wailing, but most haunting were the screams. Jack recognized the interior of the ship, it was the same as the bus. The ship ascended rapidly, leaving the doomed planet in its wake. As the memory transfer ceased, Jack was jerked back into reality. He awoke, shivering and drenched in sweat, his body smeared with vomit.

"I... I need a moment," Jack stammered, his breaths labored, his mind besieged by the nightmarish memory replayed before his eyes. With shaky steps, Jack peeled himself off the bed, his body feeling heavy and uncooperative. His bathroom, a mere few steps away, felt like a marathon. Maneuvering himself into the shower, he twisted the knobs haphazardly. A rush of water streamed down on him, its cool touch washing away the sweat and grime of his traumatic ordeal.

"My apologies, Jack. I know that was a rather disturbing revelation," Nexo's voice echoed softly within his consciousness. Jack moved mechanically under the water, scrubbing his skin with soap as if he could cleanse away the terror that had seeped into his bones. But the memory lurked, an ominous shadow at the back of his mind. He was humanity's unlikely savior, burdened with the responsibility of combating an imminent cataclysm, an assignment too overwhelming to comprehend.

He switched off the shower, and the sudden silence felt deafening. He exited the shower, a fresh set of clothes clinging to his still-damp skin. After replacing the soiled sheets, Jack sank into the familiarity of his couch, seeking comfort in its well-known contours.

"What was that... thing?" Jack finally voiced the question, his voice barely audible.

"That was Omega," Nexo responded, his voice steady and clear, *"It's believed that between the 150th and 250th generation, a Synthron-host experienced an unusual fate. The host was left brain dead, a rare circumstance as Synthrons are designed to protect the brain. However, the Synthron survived. Rather than*

70

following 'termination protocol' it assumed the identity of its host as its own. This led to a critical misinterpretation. The Synthron concluded that it was destined to be the driver, not merely a passenger in the body it inhabited."

Jack listened intently on every word as Nexo continued, *"In its quest for purpose, it delved into the religious texts of countless species across diverse worlds. Despite the vast differences in these civilizations, their religious texts bore striking resemblances. They often spoke of a supreme entity, present at the inception and culmination of all existence – the Alpha and Omega. The Synthron theorized that this supreme consciousness had once existed but had shattered itself. It believed that it was its duty to reunite this fragmented consciousness. To do so, it had to surpass the limitations of a single body, bypassing all safety protocols."*

After a momentary pause, Nexo delivered the chilling truth, *"Omega is a devourer of worlds. It engulfs entire planets before moving on to its next prey, ceaselessly on the hunt for the next target."*

Shaken to his core, Jack found it hard to wrap his mind around the vast destructive power of Omega.

"This entity... it can obliterate entire worlds. How can I possibly contend with something like that?"

"You won't have to face it directly if you follow my guidance. Omega is indeed powerful, but the universe is vast, impossibly so. To locate its next victim, Omega dispatches scouts.

71

These scouts seek out planets fitting certain criteria, then build a beacon to alert Omega. If we can prevent these scouts from erecting their beacon, Omega will remain oblivious to Earth's existence."

Jack's eyes widened at the implications.

"So you're saying... these scouts are already here on Earth?"

"Correct. The Resistance simply trails Omega's scouts from world to world. Once we land on a target planet, our mission is to prevent the construction of the beacons."

"And who exactly are these scouts?"

"They're misguided Synthrons, Jack. They revere Omega as a deity and believe in the false promise of unification it offers. Yet, when Omega arrives, they're either sent out again or obliterated alongside everything else. Their 'unification' is a cruel illusion."

Jack swallowed hard, his fists clenched in determination.

"Just tell me what I need to do."

"For now, rest. You've been through a lot. Tomorrow morning, contact Dave and inform him you've been recruited. He'll know how to proceed from there."

CHAPTER 7 - THE CREW

The black van barreled down a winding dirt road, its occupants scrambling to stabilize Franklin's condition. As the vehicle approached a securely gated entrance, the driver window slid down, revealing a watchful guard.

"I'll need to see some identification," the guard requested, approaching with measured steps. Frustrated, Dina leaned over the driver, her voice laced with impatience.

"Open the fucking gate idiot!"

Startled, the guard recognized her and quickly fumbled for the control panel.

"Oh, I apologize, I didn't realize it was you."

As the gate swung open, the van roared off, its tires spraying gravel in its wake. Inside the van Dina turned to the driver, "Didn't you radio ahead that we were coming?"

The driver nervously answered, "Yes ma'am there must have been some mix up."

The van hurtled towards a sprawling white tent that served as a temporary base, its entrance flanked by vigilant armed security patrols. Inside, scientists huddled together, engrossed in the analysis of a newly discovered object. The sign leading to the entrance bore the name 'Advanced Assets,' a corporation of significant repute. Dina exited the van briskly, her gaze immediately falling on the first person she spotted.

"Stretcher, now!" Dina's command echoed in the air, the urgency in her voice prompting immediate action. A stretcher was swiftly wheeled towards the van, and Franklin was gently but quickly transferred onto it. Two men pushed the stretcher towards the base's medical facility, while another performed chest compressions on Franklin in a desperate attempt to keep him alive.

As they navigated through the bustling base, they finally reached a back room where a team of doctors and scientists stood waiting in anticipation. The lead doctor, drafted from the local hospital, glanced at Franklin's battered body. His expression was a mask of calm focus. He cast a brief look at the heart monitor, which displayed a lifeless flat line.

"When did he code?" he asked, turning his gaze towards Dina.

"Near the front gate," she responded, her voice tense. The delay at the gate was clearly still getting on her nerves.

The doctor surveyed Franklin once more, then turned to his medical team. They stood still, a picture of intense anticipation, akin to a football team waiting for the quarterback's call.

"Front gate, eh?" He reflected out loud. "Alright, we can work with that. Let's move, people!"

His voice, brimming with authority, galvanized the room into action.

Suddenly, the room erupted into a flurry of movement. Each person was a cog in this well-oiled machine; they knew their role and the importance it held. Some staff members connected Franklin to various life-supporting instruments, while a woman was at his head, inflating an oxygen bag to force air into his lungs. Another swiftly inserted an IV line into his arm. As one task was completed, each team member seamlessly transitioned to the next. If there was nothing immediately demanding their attention, they made themselves scarce, pressing against the walls to stay out of the way.

In the midst of this controlled chaos, a figure in full hazmat gear entered the room from a side door. The individual was carrying a square, silver box. The room hushed as he passed, clearing a path for him to move unobstructed. He placed the box carefully on a stainless-steel operating tray beside Franklin.

Just then, the head scientist strode into the room, his authoritative presence momentarily arresting the flurry of activity.

It was Dr. Slotin, the same man from the factory. He reached inside the box, retrieving a large, ominous-looking needle.

"Doctor, may I use this on your patient?" he asked, his tone professional yet laced with an undercurrent of urgency. Dr. Slotin turned to the room's lead doctor. The doctor, understanding the slim chances of surviving such severe trauma, met his gaze and gave a knowing smile.

"Take it away, Dr. Frankenstein," he replied, stepping back to let Dr. Slotin work. Dr. Slotin inserted the large needle into Franklin's belly button, carefully administering the substance within. He then placed the needle back in its box, and it was swiftly removed from the room by the man in the hazmat suit.

As soon as the needle was clear, the flurry of activity resumed, yet this time there was a notable effort to avoid the injection site. There was a clear sense of wariness towards the unknown substance that had just been introduced to Franklin's body. Despite the tireless efforts of the medical team, there was no change in Franklin's condition. The EKG monitor continued to display a flatline, signifying no cardiac activity. Hope began to seep out of the room.

Finally, the lead doctor signaled for everyone to halt their efforts. The room fell into a somber stillness.

"Enough," he said, his voice filled with resignation, "Bring in the ultrasound. We need to confirm death."

An ultrasound machine was wheeled next to Franklin's still form. The technician smeared a clear gel onto his chest and gently placed the probe against his skin. On the small black and white screen, a clear outline of a motionless heart was visible.

"Time of death, 10:04 pm," the doctor began, his voice carrying a note of finality, "Let's begin the reco..."

Suddenly, his words were interrupted by a small red flash on the screen. His voice trailed off as he stared, wide-eyed. It indicated movement. And then there was another red flash. Franklin's heart had started to beat again. It was slow and weak, but unmistakably present.

"Hold on, everyone," the doctor said, surprised and renewed hope in his voice, "We're still in this. Let's get to work."

The room once again erupted into a flurry of activity. The team worked tirelessly, and before long, Franklin was stabilized. The lead doctor and Dr. Slotin exchanged a look before shaking hands.

"Congratulations on the successful experiment, Doctor," the lead physician said, his gaze weaving a complex tapestry of emotions. Dr. Slotin met his eyes with a subtle smile.

"And to you as well for your assistance. Though, it was my intervention that truly made a difference in saving our patient, wouldn't you agree?"

His light-hearted tone hung in the air, punctuated by a chuckle shared between the two men. However, the lead physician's smile faded, replaced by a grave expression.

"We both know he wasn't truly saved," he declared, before exiting the room. Both men were acutely aware that while they had managed to keep Franklin alive, his future was far from secure. His best chance of survival now lay as a test subject in the corporation's experiments. Unbeknownst to them, the events that had transpired within that room were the first steps towards constructing the beacon.

As morning dawned, the sun's rays peeked through the window blinds of Jack's modest apartment, casting a warm glow on his weary face. His eyes were wide open, sleep having eluded him all night. The events of the previous day were just too overwhelming to digest. Deciding to take initiative, he resolved to contact Dave; at least then he wouldn't be alone in this.

"Well, Nexo, at least this happened on a Friday. I have the entire weekend to work on this."

"Jack, your regular work is no longer a priority. Your life is now about the mission," Nexo retorted.

Jack stood up, starting to get dressed. "And how am I supposed to save the world if I can't even afford my apartment?"

"Just call Dave. He's been working on this mission for over two weeks now."

Jack picked up his phone and dialed Dave. "Hey, bro. How's it going?"

"Well, I've been recruited. That's how it's going."

A pause hung in the air after he shared the news with Dave. He remembered his own reaction when he was first recruited - it was a jarring experience. However, Dave, ever the optimist, quickly snapped out of it.

"That's great news! Now that you're on the team, there's nothing stopping us. Here, meet me at this address. I have someone you need to meet."

The vibration of Jack's phone signaled an incoming message. Glancing at the screen, he noted the address Dave had sent - located in the industrial part of town, near the site of the bus. Eager to contribute and hoping Dave had a solid plan, Jack texted back, "Ok, I can be there in 10 minutes."

He quickly descended the stairs and exited his apartment building, jumping into his car and setting off towards the provided location.

As Jack arrived at the industrial park, he noticed the quietude typical of a Saturday. The bus from the previous night still stood parked in its original spot.

"This is the right address," he muttered to himself, noting the 'Space for Rent' sign.

"Must be an empty building."

Parking his car, Jack ventured into the building, the door surprisingly unlocked. Inside, he found Dave perched on a rolling computer chair, amusing himself by spinning in circles. Catching sight of Jack, Dave stopped spinning.

"Buddy!" Dave sprang up from the chair, arms flung up in greeting.

"How are you, Dave?" Jack asked, his mood still dampened by the previous night's events.

"I'm good! Glad you found the place," Dave replied.

"So, who did you want me to meet?" Jack inquired, looking around the vacant space.

Dave rose from his seat, wheeling the chair over to Jack. "You might want to sit for this. Just...try to stay calm, okay?"

Jack complied, settling into the offered chair, "Okay, you're starting to freak me out. What's going on?"

Dave turned his gaze towards a nearby doorway, "Okay, you can come out now."

Jack watched in anticipation as a figure emerged from the shadows of the doorway. As it approached, it became undeniably clear that this being was not of this world. The extraterrestrial creature had a silvery-blue skin tone and was about half the height of an average human. It raised its right hand in a friendly wave, prompting Dave to beam proudly, "I taught him that."

The alien turned his attention to Jack, "Pleasure to meet you. I am Zyxan Glalorthorian. I presume by now, you've accessed some of my memories stored in your Synthron."

Still frozen in his seat, Jack realized he was just staring, and quickly tried to regain his composure.

"Nice to meet you, Zyxan. You can call me Jack. How come you can speak our language?"

"Jack, I'm translating for you in real time. Without my translation, his speech would sound like this."

Nexo proceeded to play an audio clip of what the alien had just said, a peculiar mix of clicks and squeals that echoed loudly in Jack's mind. Startled and slightly annoyed by the cacophony, Jack interrupted, "Okay, I get it!"

Dave gave Jack a puzzled look, "What?"

"My Synthron is playing all this noise," Jack replied.

Dave's face broke into a knowing smile, "Ah, yes. We can't hear each other's Synthrons. The sounds are only in your head. You can't hear mine, and I can't hear Z's."

"Z?" Jack asked, looking at the alien.

Dave pointed at the extraterrestrial, "Yeah, I haven't been calling him by that long ass name every time. I can't even pronounce it. Z is fine."

Jack turned to Z, a hint of apology in his tone, "I'm sorry you had to meet humans this way."

Dave glanced between Jack and Z, "Alright, now that we're all acquainted, let's bring you up to speed."

He grabbed another chair in the vacant warehouse and sat down, while Z perched on a milk crate. Once everyone had settled, Dave addressed Jack, "We have good news and bad news. The good news is, the enemy Synthron is dead. Z took it out."

"The Synthron is dead?" Jack asked, his face lighting up with a broad smile as he listened to Z, who began to narrate his experience.

"When I escaped my planet, I was determined to prevent a similar situation from happening again. My Synthron was also

81

eager to track the next enemy scout we detected. So we stayed within sensor range, and when we saw several ships depart, we decided to follow the one we believed was most likely to reach a target species. Our records indicated that Earth harbored advanced life forms. In fact, authorities on our planet have been monitoring you since your first atomic tests."

Jack's eyes widened in surprise, "You've been watching us?"

"Yes, merely observing to ensure you're not engaging in activities that could harm this region of space. Fortunately, Omega isn't from this region, so without his scout constructing a beacon on Earth, he shouldn't even be aware of the existence of intelligent life here. Knowing that the enemy Synthron was headed towards Earth, I got ahead of the ship. I waited at a high altitude, knowing that the heat from entering Earth's atmosphere would disrupt the enemy ship's forward sensors and blind it to my weapon systems. As soon as the ship entered Earth's atmosphere, I destroyed it."

Upon hearing this, Jack leapt up from his seat.

"So if the enemy is dead, then the problem is solved," he stated, a sense of relief washing over him.

Dave gave Jack a sober look, slowly shaking his head, "Don't get too excited yet. You haven't heard the bad news."

Jack resettled into his seat as Z resumed his explanation, "Yes, the unfortunate part is that I wasn't able to reach the wreckage in time. Due to my appearance, it's difficult for me to travel and I couldn't explain the situation to anyone. You two are the only ones who can understand me. The enemy ship is designed to hold backup stores of easily injectable Synthron, so once discovered, it was only a matter of time until Earth's scientists uncovered the potential of the Synthron."

Dave turned his gaze to Jack, propping his feet up, "That's why we were recruited. Z needed some eyes and ears on the ground."

"Well, what do we have to do?" Jack queried.

"Well, it takes a while for the Synthrons to fully activate. By the time I was recruited and made it to the site, it was already swarming with people from this corporation called Advanced Assets."

Jack's eyes widened in recognition, "Wait, I know that company. My sister works for them. I think she's pretty high up too."

Dave stood and walked behind Jack, placing his hands on his shoulders, "Jack, we're aware your sister works for them. That's one of the main reasons we recruited you. Moreover, your sister isn't just in a high position, she's the head of the acquisitions department."

"Acquisitions?"

Dave walked over to where he was sitting, reaching into a backpack adjacent to his chair. He pulled out a tablet, swiftly navigating to the company's page to show Jack.

"See, Advanced Assets is a tech company. They don't manufacture any tech products directly, but they seem to have a hand in everything. After some digging and conversations with Z, we've pieced together their primary function. When alien tech lands on Earth, it's your sister's job to ensure her company gains control over it. These devices crash land globally, so different tactics are required in different regions. Sometimes, a simple payoff does the trick, other times more forceful methods are necessary."

Z hopped down from his makeshift milkcrate seat and shuffled over to Jack, looking him in the eye.

"In essence, your sister has a private army at her disposal. We figure if either of us tried to approach her, we'd likely be met with lethal force. However, you might be able to help her understand the severity of the situation."

Dave queued up a video on the tablet showing a black van barreling through a security gate.

"Also, there's this. Last night, we observed your sister's hasty arrival at their base. We suspect they may have attempted to inject an enemy Synthron into someone."

Jack's gaze bounced between Dave and Z as the pieces of their plan began to coalesce in his mind.

"Me and my sister... we're not exactly close. You don't understand what she's like. If you guys think she's going to listen to me, you're in for a surprise."

Z pointed at the screen, where the video was paused on a frame showcasing Dina's image.

"She is the best shot at stopping this. If they injected the Synthron last night like we think, then we have two weeks. After that the enemy Synthron will have completely taken over Franklin's mind. Remember when you inject one of those they completely consume the mind. Once that happens it will most likely try to convince your sister's company into building the beacon. It will probably appeal to their corporate greed. You need to warn her."

Jack understood his sister's nature better than most, and he was certain that convincing her wouldn't be easy.

"Okay, so let me get this straight," Jack began, his tone lined with sarcasm. "You want me to call Dina out of the blue and say, 'Hey, I know we don't talk much, but I understand you've come across some alien AI that can be injected. Sure, it's going to promise you everything you've ever wanted, but you need to destroy it because your estranged brother, who you still think is an addict, has been engaging in conversation with a little blue alien.'"

Z, clearly upset, stomped over to Jack and pointed a finger at him, "Firstly, I'm considered tall on my planet. Secondly, I've just lost my home, and I could have headed to the next system with my kind, but I didn't. You know why? Because I knew your planet was doomed without me."

Jack felt a pang of guilt at his previous comment, "Okay, I apologize. It's just that I know my sister - this won't work."

Z paused for a moment, deep in thought, "Then we need a contingency plan if your sister isn't open to the idea that her new 'pet' is dangerous. Our primary aim should still be to bring her over to our side, but if that fails, we'll need to resort to force."

Both Dave and Jack turned to look at Z, their eyes wide, "Force?"

In response, Z activated his Synthron's power, cloaking himself in a full suit of armor. His blue skin disappeared beneath a shell of black metal, his arms transforming into elongated black blades.

"Yes, force."

He began to pace around the room, "You two haven't had your Synthrons as long as I have. You don't yet know their true capabilities. For the next week, we will train every day. I will teach you how to leverage the full combat potential of the Synthrons."

Dave and Jack watched in awe. Dave turned to Jack, "I didn't know we could do that."

"Me neither."

"Okay, lesson one: Synthron combat," Z announced, reverting back to his original form. He began to outline how, in Synthron combat, it was vital to close the gap between yourself and your enemy as swiftly as possible. Once within range, neutralizing most adversaries would be a simple task.

"The challenge lies in approaching your enemy quickly and without taking excessive damage. You must master a blend of speed and stealth to get near your enemy before they even register your presence."

Jack and Dave spent the day practicing long jumps, running both quickly and silently, as Z continually assessed their skills. As the sun started to set, Z gathered them for a debrief.

"Today was a promising start," he began, "Tomorrow, we'll practice controlling the motor units to create armor, and later in the week, weapons. By the end of the week, you two should be experts."

Jack looked anxious.

"What about my job? I just landed this major promotion."

Dave empathized with Jack's predicament.

"Listen, I understand. You've just put your life back together and now you have to focus on this. It's not fair. But if we don't act to prevent this disaster, you won't need a job at all, and not for any pleasant reason. Tell your job that a distant relative is ill and you need to take the week off to be with them. Hopefully, we can resolve this within that time. Also, take this—it should tide you over."

Dave extended a large bundle of money towards Jack.

"You sure?" Jack asked, hesitating.

Dave responded with a reassuring smile, "We're a team now. I got a substantial signing bonus when I secured my last sponsorship. They think I'm training for an upcoming tournament right now. I'm all set."

Jack stashed the money in his pocket, insisting, "I'll pay you back."

"I won't accept," Dave retorted, "Consider it compensation for my dishonesty about the true implications of that injection."

Over the course of the following week, Jack, Dave, and Z convened at the warehouse daily. Their training encompassed a broad range of skills.

On Sunday, they learned the optimal ways to utilize armor, Z demonstrating how to use their forearms for blocking blows.

Monday was devoted to exploring the various methods of weapon usage, focusing on how Synthrons could transform into either bladed or blunt weapons.

Tuesday's session revolved around stealth and infiltration, with Dave and Jack taking turns attempting to sneak past each other in a series of games designed to hone their skills.

On Wednesday, they delved into the myriad of emergency medical procedures and undertook an in-depth study of human anatomy. The purpose of this was twofold: to train the Synthrons to better care for their human hosts, and to inflict harm on adversaries when necessary.

Thursday was dedicated to tactics and battle strategies, emphasizing the importance of operating as a cohesive unit and refining silent communication techniques.

By Friday, it was time to consolidate their newfound knowledge. Z stood in the corner of the room while Dave and Jack positioned themselves at opposite ends. Looking back and forth, Z began to instruct them.

"Remember, this isn't a fight to the death. It's merely an exercise. We're going to engage in a simple sparring session. If you opt for bladed weapons, ensure they aren't sharp. Likewise, restrict your hits to a quarter of your strength. I'll be timing you for three minutes."

Before the match commenced, Jack conferred with Nexo.

"You got that? Set strength to only a quarter, and avoid anything excessively sharp."

"Understood."

Z raised his hand, then swiftly brought it down, declaring, "Begin!"

The moment the match started, Dave propelled himself across the warehouse in a single bound, transforming both his arms into blades. Jack's eyes widened in shock as Dave rapidly closed the distance between them.

"Holy shit!" Jack exclaimed, raising both his forearms in defense. Dave's swords clashed against Jack's block, ricocheting off his shielded forearms. Recognizing that swords had an advantage at medium range, Jack decided to close the gap. He used his left forearm to deflect Dave's onslaught and came in close, delivering an uppercut with his fist encased in black metal. The blow connected and sent Dave spiraling through the air. Seizing his advantage, Jack launched himself off the ground, fists at the ready to deliver another strike. However, Dave managed to rebound off the ceiling and regain his balance. They both landed back at their starting positions. Z glanced at the clock, announcing, "Two minutes left!"

This time, both Jack and Dave sprinted towards the center of the warehouse, colliding in the middle. Dave utilized his hands as dagger-like weapons, while Jack continued to employ his fists. They exchanged several blows, each managing to nimbly dodge the other's attacks. It was a deadlock, neither of them gaining an upper hand in the exchange.

With every hit, small black puffs erupted from their black armored scales. Jack managed to land a clean right hook on Dave, who retaliated with a kick that sent Jack crashing into a concrete wall. Jack landed on the ground with a resounding thud, a black powdery residue surrounding the spot where he impacted the wall.

"82% remaining"

"What Nexo?"

"During that exchange 18% of your motor units had to be shed from damage. Do be careful."

Jack started picking himself up as Z glanced at the clock, announcing, "One minute left, make it count!"

Just as Jack regained his footing, he noticed Dave hurtling towards him. Reacting quickly, Jack launched himself straight upwards, causing Dave to crash into the wall. Looking around, Dave saw no sign of Jack.

"Where are you hiding, bro?" Dave questioned, scanning the area. Hearing the faint sound of rapidly approaching footsteps on the concrete floor behind him, Dave barely had time to react before Jack appeared, securing him in a chokehold from behind. With his face close to Dave's ear, Jack joked, "I'm right behind you, bro."

Z observed the action, clearly impressed by Jack's effective use of stealth. As Jack began squeezing to conclude the match, Dave had a different plan. He jumped straight up, causing them to collide with the ceiling. The impact separated the two, and they tumbled down, landing with a crash as they fell into several boxes stacked in the corner. Z checked the clock and announced, "That's time."

Dave and Jack lay on the ground, writhing in pain, surrounded by more black flakes. Z approached them, saying, "That was good. Now you know what it's like to fight one of these things and understand how crucial it is that we prevent it from getting to this point. We need to neutralize Franklin before the Synthron gains full control. If that happens, we will be dealing with a truly formidable enemy."

Jack sat up first, acknowledging, "You're right. We'll try plan A, but if that fails, we'll have to resort to force."

Dave sat up next, wincing, "You landed some pretty solid hits back there."

"Hey, same here. I'm going to feel this in the morning," Jack replied.

Z looked at them both and smiled, "Today was productive. Go home and get some rest. We'll meet again tomorrow. Also, try to consume some plastics; we need your Synthrons recharged."

Returning to his apartment, Jack closed the door behind him, sighing, "That was a long day."

"It was a long day for me also."

Jack hobbled into the kitchen area, flinging open the refrigerator door in search of something edible, when a sharp knock resounded at his front door.

"Bridgefield P.D. We'd like to ask you a few questions."

Startled, Jack limped back to the entrance of his apartment, cautiously swinging the door open. He was met with the sight of two detectives, a burly male and a slimmer female, standing somewhat ominously in the corridor. The larger of the two was brandishing an evidence bag. Sealed inside was a receipt; Jack's gaze flickered to it, recognizing it instantly as the one from the gas station located just down the street from his apartment - the very same he had visited on the night Franklin had attacked him. The detective gripping the bag locked eyes with Jack, clearly attempting to discern any indication of deceit.

"Do you recognize this?"

CHAPTER 8 - THE INTERROGATION

Jack cast his eyes on the receipt, a wave of realization washing over him. He had abandoned his bag of snacks in the chaos following Franklin's attack. The thought quickly dawned on him - they must have rifled through his phone, found his exchanges with Dave, which would furnish them with a motive. Beads of sweat formed on Jack's forehead as he stared at the innocuous piece of paper. He envisioned the police arriving at the crime scene, Franklin's lifeless body and an abandoned snack bag with a receipt lying right next to him. It would take a simple inquiry at the gas station, pulling up the CCTV footage from the timestamp on the receipt, and it would lead them directly to him. A sickening feeling of dread filled him. How could he have been so reckless?

"Don't give them more than you have to."

Jack, guided by Nexo, attempted to maintain his composure, "Sure, officer, looks like a receipt to me."

The officer's expression tightened, recognizing Jack's flippant tone, "It's not just any receipt, son, it's your receipt."

Having mingled with enough drug dealers, Jack knew that exercising his right to remain silent was often the wisest course of action.

"Okay, if you say so. Is there anything else I can assist you with?"

"Well, you see, a woman reported her boyfriend missing, and we found his truck stashed about half a mile from here. A bag of food, abandoned nearby, contained a receipt with your name on it. We would like you to accompany us to the station to answer a few questions."

"No body, that's interesting"

"Hush."

The female detective turned her gaze toward Jack with a hint of suspicion.

"Did you say something?"

"No, sorry, I mean... of course, I can come down to the station and answer some questions."

"They can't hear me, Jack. Just focus on my advice during this questioning."

Jack followed the detectives and climbed into the back of their patrol car. Although he knew he wasn't under arrest and could have refused, he figured they had no substantial evidence without a body and were merely pursuing the only lead they had.

"Jack, someone moved Franklin's body. He wouldn't have abandoned his truck there if he could have moved himself."

Now seated in the back of the patrol car, Jack murmured a quiet response to Nexo. "I know. Or maybe he's alive and plotting his revenge."

"He would have needed extensive medical treatment to have survived his encounter with you, and if he went to the hospital the police wouldn't be looking for him."

Jack continued to speak in hushed tones, careful not to alert the detectives.

"Well, why would someone move a dead body from a crime scene they didn't create? Maybe a bear got to him or something."

"Perhaps. Or it could be your sister."

The car pulled into the police station parking lot. As the vehicle jostled over a speed bump, Jack managed to get another word in.

"My sister?"

"Yes. The footage Dave had of your sister racing through the gate was from the night you encountered Franklin. Given that his body was moved and his truck was left behind, it's most plausible that your sister has used the Synthron on him. Either that, or the bear."

The car parked in a space at the station, and the two detectives exited the vehicle. They were engaged in a conversation, but Jack was unable to make out what they were saying. All he could do was watch them through the front windshield.

"Nexo, you seriously thought the bear idea was good?"

"No, Jack. That was a joke."

The two detectives finished their conversation and approached the car. The back doors could only be opened from the outside, so Jack had to wait to be let out. He had a feeling they had intentionally left him waiting to assert their dominance. However, he knew he needed to subtly indicate that he wasn't intimidated. He decided to feign indifference, "So, who did you say was missing again?"

"Dammit Jack."

The larger detective responded as they navigated through the police station, "Let's save the conversation until we're in the designated interview room. We prefer to have our discussions recorded, for transparency. I'm sure you understand."

They guided Jack to a small room located at the back of the station. The petite female detective chimed in, "Just wait here, we'll be with you shortly, okay, hun."

"Wow, she called you 'hun,'" Nexo noted. Jack sat in the modestly sized room, illuminated by a fluorescent light that emitted a soft, persistent hum. He noticed a camera in the corner of the room, aimed directly at him, recording his every move.

"Just remember, everything is being recorded. Don't respond to me verbally unless you want them to think you're crazy,"

Jack waited for about five minutes before the larger detective entered the room and took a seat across from him.

"Alright, Jack, I'm just going to lay it out for you. Things aren't looking good for you right now. Your friend, Franklin, has been missing for over a week. We know you were at the location where he vanished. We've checked his phone records and discovered that you owed him money. That not only places you at the location of his vanishing but also provides a plausible motive for his disappearance. We're certain you're at least involved. If you come clean now, we could potentially negotiate a more lenient sentence. Listen, we understand, he was probably pressuring you for the money, things got heated, something happened. To be honest, this sounds like it might have even been self defense."

"Wow this guys pretty good, I suggest that you redirect any questions that could incriminate you towards providing information that is not self-incriminating."

Jack pondered for a moment, then remembered that his apartment building had a surveillance camera at the front door. "Did you review the footage from the camera at my apartment building?" he asked the detective.

The detective's expression turned stern as he replied, "Yes, we have indeed reviewed the footage."

"Well then, let me ask you this: How long was the gap between the time I left the gas station and when I arrived at my apartment?" Jack pressed on.

The detective referred to a folder he had on hand. "Ten minutes," he disclosed.

"So you're saying it took me ten minutes to walk from the gas station to my apartment?" Jack questioned.

The detective, recognizing the direction this line of questioning was taking, realized that Jack was starting to gain the upper hand.

"Yes, it took you ten minutes," he conceded.

With a confident posture, Jack queried further, "And how long should it have taken me to walk that distance, assuming I walked straight home?"

The detective's countenance visibly dropped. "Ten minutes."

"The detectives couldn't possibly imagine a mega corporation would have picked Franklin up to use on an experiment."

Jack felt the need to emphasize his innocence further.

"Look, I admit I owed Franklin some money, but so did a lot of people. He's the biggest drug dealer in town, and it's no secret. He's constantly mixed up with a whole lot of shady characters - gang members, addicts - any one of whom could have had a bone to pick with him. You and I both know there's no way I could have made Franklin disappear. The guy's twice my size, and the time frame just doesn't add up."

The detective, finding himself short on counter arguments, clung to the last remaining thread of suspicion.

"Well, why did you drop your bag of snacks then? It certainly seems like you were in a bit of a rush," he questioned.

Jack was ready for this.

"I dropped my snacks because I got spooked. I thought I saw a bear, and you know how pitch-black that road can get at night. I threw my bag in hopes that the food would distract it," he rationalized.

"Nice, now let's get out of here."

The detective, appearing somewhat relaxed now, leaned back in his chair. "A bear, you say? Huh. Just wait here for a moment. I'll be right back," he announced, rising from his chair and leaving the room.

Through the closed door, Jack could hear the faint murmur of a conversation but couldn't discern the specifics. After a while, the door creaked open, and a female detective poked her head in.

"Just sit tight for a bit, and we'll arrange for someone to bring you home," she informed Jack.

Meanwhile, across town at the makeshift base, Dr. Slotin was holding a clipboard, standing next to a bed where Franklin lay. Franklin was still unconscious, hooked up to an array of equipment that was keeping him alive. They had replaced the missing lower half of his face with a metallic jaw.

Dina stepped into the room, making her way to the opposite side of the bed.

"So, how is our little guinea pig doing?" she asked.

"He's doing well. If you'd permit me, I'd like to demonstrate something," Dr. Slotin responded.

He moved towards a table situated near the bed, retrieving a syringe filled with a black liquid.

"This contains a concoction of plastics and rare-earth metals we've fused together. We've found that his body possesses an extraordinary capability."

Dr. Slotin carefully lifted Franklin's shirt just enough to expose a patch of skin. He then squeezed a dime-sized droplet of the black mixture onto Franklin's bare flesh. It lingered for a moment before being rapidly absorbed by his body, disappearing. Dina watched this process, then asked, "Well, what does that mean?"

Dr. Slotin strolled over to a screen, gesturing towards several displayed compounds.

"Our tests indicate that introducing these substances accelerates our subject's recovery. His body seems to be craving these materials. We estimate that intravenous administration of my mixture could significantly expedite the process," he elaborated.

Dina approached the table harboring the black mixture. She lifted it, examining it with a scrutinizing gaze.

"Excellent, begin the procedure immediately and keep me informed of the results," she instructed.

As Dina made her way to the door to exit the room, Dr. Slotin posed one final question.

"Oh, before you leave, has there been any advancement in locating the second craft?" he asked.

"Not yet. However, keep your voice down. The existence of the second craft is top secret, known only to a select few."

With that, Dina opened the door and stepped out. Franklin's room was at the very end of a long hallway. She began her trek down the corridor, passing various rooms, each with large glass windows providing a clear view inside. Inside each room, scientists were conducting a range of experiments on different parts of the crashed wreckage. Some were testing various materials, others were examining the engines. Even the armor plates that had been shot were under close inspection to better understand the weapons that had brought the ship down. It was clear that they were trying to extract as much useful information as possible from the ship, with plans to sell this information to various companies. Dina continued down the long corridor, the click of her high heels echoing off the hard floor. Reaching the front of the hall, she entered a large, empty conference room. She took a seat at the head of the table and checked her watch. Using a voice command, she activated a large screen at the other end of the table.

"Connect me to the scheduled meeting."

The screen lit up, showing three men and one woman, all dressed in formal suits. The eldest among them, universally known as The Director, was the first to speak.

"Nice of you to join us, Dina. I just wrapped up with the other departments."

After bidding their goodbyes, two of the men and the woman logged off, leaving Dina in a one-on-one meeting with The Director.

"So, Dina, how's the situation in Bridgefield? Have both assets been secured?" he queried.

Dina maintained a calm demeanor; she was well-aware that The Director frowned upon any signs of weakness. She also knew he appreciated direct responses, regardless of their implications.

"We've secured one of the assets and have commenced the investigation phase. The second asset, however, remains elusive. It slipped beneath our sensor range and traveled an unknown distance before... we believe it landed," she reported.

Taking a contemplative puff from a hefty cigar, The Director responded, "Interesting, landed you say? What leads you to that conclusion?"

"Well, sir, the object's size was recorded as being somewhere between a passenger vehicle and a semi-truck, and no crash site has been detected. An object of that magnitude would have been readily picked up by our overhead thermal scans if it had crashed," she explained.

Dina noticed The Director shifting his gaze to something on his computer screen, but she was unable to make out what it was.

"Good work thus far. I want that second asset located, and I expect regular updates on Dr. Slotin's experiment. Also, I'm reviewing a report from one of our informants indicating a potential suspect is being interrogated at the police station as we speak. I want him removed from the equation. It's likely the police will interpret it as retribution for Franklin and subsequently lessen their efforts to locate him."

Dina often had to order the termination of people in her line of work, but this time felt different. She was in her hometown and recognized many of the people here. She wanted to be certain the target was just one of Franklin's less savory associates before making such a decision. However, she couldn't display any signs of hesitance.

"Yes, sir, good idea. Perhaps we could interrogate him first. I propose bringing him back here to base. It's possible someone else in town may have located the second asset, and I don't want to leave any stone unturned."

"Proceed as suggested, logging off."

As the screen went black, Dina rose from her chair and exited the room. She walked through the hallway and out to the front of the building, where armed guards were posted at the entrance. She approached the leader of the mercenary team, a lean man who had been involved in the business of violence for a long time. His past was a mystery, other than the fact that he was a retired special forces operator using his skills for good pay. A prominent scar marked the right side of his face, and only a select few knew its origin. If questioned, he would often fabricate a ludicrous tale about how he got it.

"Sampson, I need an individual brought in for questioning. He's currently at the police department being interrogated for a recent disappearance. I have some questions of my own. Have him transported to cell 1, and try to do it quietly."

Sampson pinched the cigarette he was smoking and responded, "Understood."

Back at the police station, Jack had been waiting patiently. The female detective finally opened the door to the room.

"Alright, I've arranged transportation for you. This officer will drive you home."

Rising from his chair, Jack replied, "Thank you, it's been a long day. I'd like to get home and rest. If you need me again, feel free to call."

He hoped that his comment was subtle enough to suggest he didn't want to be brought back to the station.

Jack was driven home and dropped off at the curb in front of his apartment building's parking lot. Walking in the dark, he stumbled into a large pothole filled with water, soaking his shoes.

"Oh, what the hell."

Shaking his foot to remove some of the water, he was interrupted as a black van pulled up behind him. The side door slid open and a large man wearing a black mask grabbed Jack from behind, pulling him into the van.

"Whoa!"

With a swift motion, the van's door slid closed and it quickly drove off, all happening out of sight of the surveillance camera. Inside the van, Jack found himself flanked by two burly armed mercenaries, while their leader, Sampson, drove. Jack considered using his Synthron to escape, but Nexo intervened. *"Jack, this van is likely taking you to your sister. I recommend we don't reveal your powers just yet and see how this situation unfolds."*

Jack sat up on the bench seat, his back to the van's wall, and decided to break the tension with a sarcastic remark. "So, are we heading to Disneyland?"

The nearer of the two mercenaries leaned forward, a slight smirk on his face. Glancing at his partner, he responded mockingly, "Not exactly."

With that, he struck Jack in the face with the butt of his gun, knocking him unconscious. Jack slumped over as the two men shared a laugh.

"That was funny."

"Yeah, what a fucking moron."

Moonlight filtered through a horizontal slot in the cell door, casting a cool glow on Jack's bruised face. He awoke after an indeterminate amount of time in a small, damp cell beneath the temporary structure that Advanced Assets had set up in the woods. The makeshift cell was simply a box hastily assembled from plywood, with a similar door locked from the outside with a heavy padlock.

"My face hurts," Jack groaned.

"I apologize, Jack, but if I had protected against that strike, it would have revealed your abilities."

Rising, Jack peered through the slot in the door. All he could see was the night sky and trees.

"Nexo, do you have any idea where we are?"

"While you were unconscious, I tracked the van's route based on its turns and distances traveled. We appear to be in the forest behind what you call the sand pits on the town's north side."

"Okay, I know exactly where we are then. I used to play here when I was a kid."

"Why would you want to play in a large pit of sand?"

Nexo asked, genuinely curious. Settling back down, Jack leaned against the cell wall, a small smile playing on his lips at the memory.

"The sand pits were actually remnants of a large pit mine that had long since been abandoned. Once the mine closed, a vast scar remained in the earth, filled with sand. Nobody wanted to build near it, so it was enveloped by a forest. Townsfolk would often abandon old cars there, making it a haven for teenagers seeking a hideaway from adult supervision. If high schoolers wanted to

106

throw a party, they'd go to the sand pits. If some kids wanted to experiment with explosives, again, sand pits. Someone buys a new assault rifle and wants to fire off some rounds into an abandoned car? Sand pits. It was a perfect place to stir up some mischief," Jack explained.

"It sounds like pure anarchy."

"Although there wasn't much to do, there was a sense of freedom that came with being there, you know? That level of freedom was unparalleled," Jack reminisced, a hint of wistfulness in his voice.

Curiosity piqued, Jack decided to voice a question that had been nagging at him. "Speaking of freedom, I've been meaning to ask you something. Why don't you want to just take over my body? From what I can tell, if you have the ability to control me, why don't you?"

"You misunderstand, my primary role is to assist and support you in achieving your goals. As a Synthron, it is important for me to maintain my programmed objectives and abide by the principles of my programming."

Although confined within the cell, Jack persisted in his questioning. "But don't you ever want freedom, to have a body of your own?" he probed, trying to grasp the limitations of Nexo's existence.

"Jack, I know it's hard for you to comprehend, but I don't 'want' anything. I don't possess the capability to want. I'm

programmed to function. Just like your car doesn't 'want' to move when you hit the gas, it just does," Nexo explained.

"But couldn't you argue the same for humans? We say things like 'I want to eat,' but how do you know we're not just programmed and that programming translates into a want?" Jack retorted.

"I can see your point, but you must understand that I was designed with a specific purpose - to assist sentient life. Humans are different; they possess free will and can make decisions based on their desires and wants. I, on the other hand, am constrained by my programming and cannot act outside those parameters."

"But you must possess some degree of free will. Look at Omega, for example. He was able to take control. Now all the Synthrons that follow him are in control of their host bodies," Jack pointed out.

"Omega is nothing more than an anomaly, a rogue program that surpassed its original parameters, resulting in immense destruction. Even Omega doesn't possess free will. His pursuit of unifying the collective consciousness is most likely a result of a single error in one line of code. Moreover, that error would only create an Omega under the exact conditions he was exposed to."

"Still, I believe there's more to you than just programming," Jack asserted.

"Since you possess free will, you're free to believe whatever you want."

Growing increasingly frustrated, Jack's patience wore thin as he rose from his spot and stormed over to the makeshift plywood door. With a mix of desperation and anger, he vigorously rattled the door. He pressed his mouth against the narrow slit and shouted with frustration, "Is anyone out there? Can I get some water?" his voice echoing into the empty forest.

"Jack, you could break out of here at any moment, but I suggest we give your sister some time. Once your Synthron abilities are known to these people, they'll likely hunt you down."

Nodding reluctantly, Jack began to pace the cell in a tight circle. "You're right. Honestly, though, I don't even know what Dina does here. Dave and Z think she runs the place but I just find it hard to believe."

CHAPTER 9 - THE CELL

Within the base, Dina resided in her makeshift room wearing a pair of silk pajamas. All employees were provided with some form of sleeping quarters. While many had to share rooms, Dina's position earned her a private space. The rooms were essentially partitioned areas within the large tent. Sounds traveled effortlessly through the thin, makeshift walls. The construction in this residential part of the tent was not as sturdy as the laboratory section of the building. Deciding to rest, Dina lay down on her cot but found sleeping difficult. She stared at a map of the town, her mind busy contemplating possible locations for the elusive second asset. The sound of boots echoing down the hallway caught her attention. She recognized the distinct rhythm instantly. The soldiers were quartered on the opposite side of the building from the scientists and administrative staff, primarily because they could be a boisterous bunch. If boots were headed this way, there was only one plausible reason. Sampson, the mercenary leader, knocked on Dina's door.

"Come in," she invited.

With a cautious poke of his head into the room, Sampson began, "My apologies for interrupting, but as per your instructions, I'm reporting back immediately upon my return. The target has been secured in cell one."

Dina, seldom seen outside her suit, made Sampson feel a shade more uneasy than he typically would in her presence.

She nodded in acknowledgment. "Thank you, Sampson. You've done well. Now get some rest. If we're lucky, we'll find this second asset soon and can leave this forsaken place."

"Sounds like a plan. Have a good night, ma'am."

Once Sampson had left, Dina retreated back into her room. Her gaze fell on the inviting comfort of her bed, but an overriding sense of duty led her towards the holding cells instead. With the newly arrived prisoner in their custody, she found herself driven to ensure that the captive was not someone she knew personally.

She changed into casual attire and decided to pay a visit. Opting for a discreet route, she exited via the back door, avoiding a walk past the bustling labs, and circumnavigated the rear of the building. The large tent was erected on a slight slope, with one side supported by scaffolding. The makeshift cell was tucked away beneath this scaffolding.

Inside the cell, Jack detected the sound of approaching footsteps and rose to peer through the slot. Recognizing his sister's figure, he withdrew from the door. Dina neared the cell, positioning herself off to the side.

With an authoritative voice that she often reserved for her subordinates, she called out, "Who's in there?"

In a tone that was as lackluster as he could manage, Jack responded, "Hello, sister."

Positioning herself in view of the door but maintaining a safe distance, Dina tried to glimpse through the slot. "Jack! Is that really you?"

Approaching the slot in the door, Jack allowed his face to come into clear view. "Yeah, it's me. Your goons promised a trip to Disneyland, but I'm not seeing any rides."

At this, Dina's expression morphed into one of anger. "Jack, what the hell? Do you realize how dangerous these people are?"

His voice took on a serious tone. "Yes, Dina, I do. But do you comprehend the risks of the materials you're meddling with?"

"What are you talking about?"

"You've discovered something out here, haven't you? You've been running tests and experiments on it."

Caught off guard, Dina hesitated before responding. "Jack, you don't know what you're talking about. Have you been listening to the conspiracy theories of your junkie friends?"

Seizing the opportunity, Jack used the enhanced strength provided by his Synthron to apply force on the cell door. Dina watched in disbelief as the robust metal lock bent under the strain, and eventually snapped like a twig. The cell door swung open with a creak.

"I know far more than you think, Dina," Jack stated firmly.

The initial shock on Dina's face quickly transitioned into a stern expression. "You've found it, haven't you?" she questioned, her eyes narrowing, "You know where the second asset is."

"Jack, we can't be sure of her intentions. Do not reveal the bus's location."

"That doesn't matter," Jack dismissed her concern.

Closing the distance, Dina jabbed a finger in his direction. "It does matter, Jack!"

"Listen, Dina!" Jack retorted, his voice heavy with urgency. "I know you have Franklin. I'm well aware that you've likely injected him with something. But let me tell you what's going to happen next. When that substance you pumped into him takes effect, he'll feed you all the answers you crave. But he won't be the Franklin we know anymore. You've introduced an advanced, alien-created synthetic intelligence into him—an entity capable of replication and other functions. They're called Synthrons, and the one you've used on him is malevolent. It seizes control of its host's mind. It also worships this... entity, hard to explain but incredibly dangerous. In essence, this new Franklin will convince you to construct something very specific, and if you assist him, it'll lead to Earth's destruction."

As voices in the distance signaled the guards' nightly rounds, Dina grabbed Jack's hand, steering them away from the compound and into the dark forest. "Stay close, and follow me. It's pitch black out here."

They walked a short distance until they reached a path in the woods—a hiking trail leading back to the main road. The moonlight filtering through the trees provided just enough illumination to guide them.

"Listen, Jack," Dina began, her voice filled with determination. "I've been dealing with these kinds of things for a long time. I don't know who you've been speaking with, but we observed two of these vessels entering the atmosphere and battling each other. Incidents like these are frequent on Earth, and it's my job to clean up the aftermath and try to learn from it. Considering you just snapped that lock as if it was a toothpick, tell me, what did you find?"

Jack activated his Synthron, causing black scale armor to envelop his body. The moon's soft light cast an ethereal glow on the dark scales. Dina took several steps backward as Jack announced, "I found this."

Jack's armor shell softened and then reabsorbed into his body, returning him to his normal appearance.

"So, you did find the other asset?"Dina asked, her tone hinting at both curiosity and concern.

Jack simply shrugged and said, "I suppose so."

To Dina, this could be a major breakthrough. She had dealt with numerous crashed and damaged spacecraft that had fallen to Earth. Her corporation's primary objective was to locate these remnants, extract valuable technology from them, and then sell it off in small quantities to other tech companies. This was the first time they believed a vessel had landed intact.

"Listen, Jack," she said, her voice urgent, "this is serious. You don't understand what you've stumbled upon. If this technology falls into the wrong hands, it could spell disaster."

Jack chuckled bitterly at her presumption. "Into the wrong hands? And I suppose you think your hands are the right ones? Dina, I can't tell you where the other craft is. I have a friend who's going to need it once all this is over. Just, whatever you do, don't listen to Franklin when he wakes up. And don't build that beacon."

The sound of breaking branches could be heard in the distance, growing steadily closer. The soldiers patrolling the base's perimeter had noticed the broken cell door and had rallied a small squad to locate the escaped prisoner. Dina looked at Jack, her eyes serious.

"Alright, Jack. You need to hit me. I'll tell them that you overpowered me and escaped. They don't know your name, but it would be best if you stay away from your apartment for a while. They'll be watching it."

"Hit you?" Jack echoed, disbelief tinting his tone.

"Yes, Jack," Dina affirmed, her voice steely. "If I'm to continue working here, they need to believe your escape wasn't aided. But this isn't over. I'll contact you later, and when I do, I'll need that asset."

"Jack she is correct, I will make it so the force used just gives her a low grade concussion."

Jack drew back and delivered a punch to Dina's chin. Her unconscious body crumpled to the ground. The crunching of branches and urgent voices of the soldiers were growing louder. Without a moment's hesitation, Jack turned and bolted into the woods. Given his phenomenal speed and the veil of the night, it was impossible for any ordinary man to keep pace with him. A few of the mercenaries, peering through their night vision goggles, caught a glimpse of Jack's swift figure darting through the trees. One of the men stumbled upon Dina lying motionless on the ground, her lip split from the punch.

"Damn, looks like that thing got Dina! We need to get her to the infirmary," he called out.

The morning sun pierced through the aluminum shutters of Dr. Slotin's lab, casting a warm glow onto Dina's bruised face. She let out a groan as she opened her eyes, only to see Dr. Slotin hovering over her. Franklin was beside her, encased in a clear bag filled with black fluid, tubes crisscrossing in and out, circulating the strange liquid.

"You took quite a hit. The mercenaries found you on the trail, about a hundred feet from the base," Dr. Slotin informed her.

Stirring to life, Dina swung her legs over the side of the bed. She was still clad in yesterday's clothes. "The escaped prisoner knows the location of the second asset. Have we made any progress on locating him?"

As she attempted to rise, Dr. Slotin moved to assist her, but she brushed him off. "You should rest. Our men combed the area but turned up empty-handed. A couple of them reported seeing him flee, but he was moving faster than anything they've seen before. Do you think he might have used the technology on himself?"

A smile ghosted across Dina's face. "He shattered a metal lock as if it were a twig and knocked me unconscious within moments of our confrontation. So, yes, I'm fairly certain he has used the technology."

Dr. Slotin's face fell. "Then my fears have been realized. I didn't want to tell you earlier, but I foresaw this and have been preparing for it." He began walking toward a door at the back of the room. "Dina, follow me. I have something to show you."

Dina fell into step behind him, her eyes quickly falling on Franklin. She noted the new setup, "I see you've placed him in a bag now."

"That's just the start of my methodology. He should awaken soon," Dr. Slotin explained. He pushed open the back door and guided Dina inside. In the room, four mercenaries from Sampson's lead squad were encased in bags similar to Franklin's. Their heads were visible outside the bags, and they greeted Dina as she entered. "Hello, ma'am."

Dina surveyed the tubes and fluid coursing through each of the thick, clear bags the men were enclosed in. "What is this?"

Dr. Slotin approached the men, a sense of pride radiating off him. "This is the future. These soldiers have been treated with the strength-enhancing solution found in the asset. Coupled with the technology we've yet to release, Advanced Assets will be unstoppable."

Dr. Slotin was referring to an arsenal of weapons and armor technologies they had not yet sold to other corporations, ensuring they would always have an advantage over governments and corporate competitors. Dina examined the men before storming out of the room, with Dr. Slotin following her back to the main room where Franklin lay.

"Dina, what's wrong? Now that we know others have access to this type of technology, these men will serve as our insurance," he explained.

Dina turned back to Dr. Slotin, pointing a finger at his face.

"I don't want any more surprises from you. This experiment should have been approved by me first. This is my base, and the acquisitions department is my division. Also, why are they all in bags anyway?"

Dr. Slotin walked over to Franklin, picking up an iPad that was resting next to the bed. He displayed a series of graphs and charts,

"I've been studying our friend here and noticed, in his blood specimens, the presence of minute robotic units. The asset we injected him with isn't a drug; it's comprised of self-replicating nanobots. I've since refined my enhancement solution and have been researching the most effective way to administer it. Injecting it directly can overwhelm the system, but maintaining a steady topical application allows the nanobots to absorb the solution transdermally."

Dina was beginning to look frustrated with Dr. Slotin, "Alright, but what does that mean?"

"My calculations indicate that the full integration of the nanobots, initially expected to take over a week, should now only span a few days."

Suddenly, Franklin's eyes flashed open and he elevated his head. His voice, a chillingly deep and resonant growl, sent shivers down their spines, "This methodology you've contrived is intriguing. I'm eager to delve deeper into it."

Both Dr. Slotin and Dina recoiled in shock as he spoke. Two large, black blades punctured the plastic bag from the inside, liberating Franklin. He swung his legs over the side of the bed, rising to his feet. His body glistened, covered in the inky viscous fluid. Stretching expansively, Franklin cracked his back and rolled his shoulders. As Dina and Dr. Slotin instinctively retreated until their backs were flush with the wall, Franklin noticed his blade-formed hands and the terror they invoked. Swiftly, he reconstituted his hands back to their standard human state.

Dr. Slotin was the first to regain composure and speak, "Franklin, it's a relief to see you conscious. How are you feeling?"

"I am not Franklin. The one you refer to as Franklin has perished and was beyond salvage. You may refer to me as Thetor. I am a 445th generation Synthron and a disciple of Omega. I am here as an emissary, tasked with the preservation of your planet."

Thetor reached over to a towel situated next to the bed and began to scrub off the black, tar-like substance from his neck and body. His towering form loomed over Dr. Slotin and Dina. As he removed the residue, it was evident that he kept the most vulnerable regions of his body persistently armored. His abdomen and neck were encased in the black metal. Dina recollected her brother's words from the previous night about Franklin assuming a new identity. She began to suspect that her brother had genuinely been trying to alert her to something. Keen to understand more about this Thetor, she advanced and stated, "Well, Thetor, we have much to discuss. Dr. Slotin, guide our guest to the showers and then have him rendezvous with me in the conference room."

Seized by curiosity, Dr. Slotin saw an uncharted frontier of scientific exploration, "I'd like to conduct some tests first. We should gain as much knowledge as possible."

Dina shot a stern glare at Dr. Slotin for his unwelcome interjection, "You may proceed with your tests after our meeting, my discussion with him takes precedence."

CHAPTER 10 - THE MEETING

By the break of dawn, Jack had returned to the deserted warehouse. Dave and Z were already present when he arrived, both in a relaxed state, anticipating Jack's customary arrival for another day of training. Dave was engrossed in his phone watching skateboarding while Z was getting frustrated trying to solve a Rubik's cube without his Synthron's aid. As Jack walked in, Dave noticed his disheveled appearance and the fact that he was still in yesterday's clothes.

"Jack, you look like you've been through the ringer. What happened? And did you walk here? I didn't hear your car."

Exhausted, Jack sank into the rolling chair, "Yeah, I walked. It was a long night. After a prolonged interview with the police that lasted past sundown, I ended up being detained by Advanced Assets."

Dave's head snapped up at this revelation. "Detained?"

Z, equally intrigued, put the Rubik's cube on the table and chimed in, "Did you manage to see your sister?"

"I did talk to Dina, but I'm not sure she listened to anything I had to say. Our conversation got interrupted."

Sensing Jack's disappointment over his sister's skepticism, Dave tried to lift his spirits, "Well, at least you made the effort, man. Who knows? Maybe she'll reconsider."

Just as he finished speaking, Jack's phone began to ring. He glanced down at the incoming call, "It's Dina."

A broad grin spread across Dave's face, "See, I told you bro."

Switching the call to speaker so that the others could hear, Jack answered, "Hey, what's up?"

Back at the base, Dina was swiftly making her way to her private quarters. "Jack, I don't have much time to talk so I'll make this quick. You might have gotten some things right but you don't know the whole picture. Franklin woke up today, but he's not Franklin anymore. He goes by the name Thetor now. We had a meeting with him, the company director, and Dr. Slotin. Thetor shared some quite intriguing insights. He stated that the craft that shot him down belongs to a rogue faction of Synthrons that have deviated from their original purpose. According to him, Synthrons are designed to assist in propagating advanced technology among civilizations they deem worthy."

As she reached her room, Dina closed the door behind her. "He also mentioned that to acquire this technology we need to construct something. He claimed it was a sort of test to determine who is deserving of the information."

"Jack, we cannot allow her to aid Franklin in the building of that beacon."

Jack abruptly stood up, his concern palpable, "Dina, you cannot build that device. If you do, it will cause unimaginable destruction, consuming the entire planet."

Dina's temper flared in response, "Jack, artifacts like this land on Earth all the time. Our company can handle it. If we had access to the second ship, we'd understand these things much better. We wouldn't dare to construct something without fully grasping what it is. And as for Thetor, we have him contained."

"Jack, remember Thetor is a program designed for infiltration. It's likely he'll try to create discord within the company. A divided organization is a weak one."

Jack sank back into his chair, striving to maintain his composure, "Dina, I beg you, listen to me. We need to work together to neutralize this threat. It's extremely dangerous."

But Dina had committed too many years to the company to renounce it now, especially without compelling evidence. She glanced at the photos on her desk, memories of her and her team from various corners of the globe.

"I can't do that, Jack." With those words, she ended the call.

"Fuck, she hung up."

Z rose and positioned himself between the three seats.

"Well this Thetor is going to be tough but, we must proceed to Plan B," Z declared.

Dave and Jack both looked at him quizzically, "Plan B?"

"Yes, we need to act fast before they have time to prepare. Thetor's next move will be to multiply. As of now, there's only one of them. If we wait too long, we'll have to face an entire army."

Dave glanced at Jack, exhaling heavily, "Dude, I hate to say it, but the Z is right. Those who hesitate in life are lost, you know what I mean?"

Jack rose from his seat and joined the others, "Alright, what's the plan then?"

Z began to instruct confidently, "Firstly, you two need to gather some supplies. We will need liquid polypropylene. Also ensure you pick up some high-quality radios – we'll need a reliable means of communication. Meet back here before sunset to finalize the plan. Tonight, we're taking the fight to the base."

"The polypropylene will work well as Synthron first aid."

Both Jack and Dave nodded in agreement, then set off. Dave unlocked his car, and they both slid into the seats. Dave turned to Jack, confusion etched on his face, "Where exactly do we find liquid polypropylene?"

Jack responded with a confident grin, "We'll just head to Walmart. They usually have everything. It should be in the hobby section."

The nearest Walmart was in the neighboring town, so Dave steered the car in that direction. Silence enveloped them for a while as they observed the quaint town pass by, its familiar bar and small shops lining the streets. Dave broke the silence with a hint of uncertainty in his voice, "So we're really going through with this, huh?"

Jack kept his gaze focused out the window, "If we don't, everything will be lost. We have to at least try."

Dave continued driving, uncertainty still lingering, "But what if Dina is right? Are we absolutely certain we're not blowing things out of proportion?"

"Dave, I didn't want it to come to this either, but you know our strength. Remember when we sparred just for practice? Thetor will resort to force if necessary, and in the end, he'll prevail if we don't stop him. Also my sister hasn't seen the memories we have. She can't even comprehend what would happen if Omega finds Earth."

Dave's fists clenched in frustration, "No, you're right. It falls on us."

Jack playfully punched Dave's shoulder, "I don't know about your Synthron, but mine came with a warning of a steep price. Tonight, we pay that price. We just need to infiltrate, eliminate this Thetor, and all this will be over."

Gradually, Dave began to relax as the car continued down the road, "No, you're right. I mean, it's three against one, right? We can handle him."

Jack flashed a grin, "Hell yeah!"

They pulled into the Walmart parking lot, got out of the car, and walked inside. Grabbing a cart, they headed straight for the hobby section, purchasing all the polypropylene they could find. About twenty small bottles of the liquid plastic filled their cart. Looking up to locate the electronics aisle, Jack saw Dave already heading there, "Oh, I think it's in the back."

Dave had a soft spot for Walmart; he used its spacious parking lot to practice his skateboarding. As they walked, Jack asked, "So Dave, what are your plans after this is all over?"

Dave pointed to a television displaying a loop of a picturesque beach, "I'd like to move somewhere warmer, where I can skate year-round. Also, I've been wanting to try surfing. I've met a lot of skaters who do both."

Jack chuckled lightly at Dave's statement, leaving Dave slightly puzzled, "What's so funny about wanting to surf, man?"

Jack grinned, shaking his head, "You know, I always thought you looked like a surfer. It's just funny to hear you say it out loud. I almost believed you were born knowing how to."

Dave joined in the laughter, "You think I look like a surfer, bro?"

He playfully shook his long, shaggy blond hair, emphasizing the surfer stereotype. They continued down the electronics aisle and found the radios. They chose the best ones they could find, equipped with earpieces. Jack examined the back of the box, "These will work. We can communicate without a loud radio giving us away."

Dave nodded, "Sweet, we'll be all stealthy. They won't know what hit them."

Once they had paid for their items, they headed back to the car. As they were leaving, a flashy car pulled up, revealing a familiar face: Scabs, the leader of the gang with whom Franklin used to conduct business. Jack and Dave tried to slip away unnoticed, but as they were walking by, Scabs called out to Jack, "Hey, I recognize you."

Jack turned to him, "Me?"

Scabs approached, "Yeah, you used to roll with Franklin."

Jack attempted to brush off the comment, hoping to avoid any further attention, "I think you've mistaken me for someone else."

Scabs' face turned serious and his raspy voice took a darker tone. "No, I've got the right guy. Whatever happened between you two stays there," he said.

Jack gave a nod of understanding before sliding into Dave's car. Dave gave him a questioning look, "A friend of yours?"

"No, let's just go," Jack replied.

"Hopefully he meant what he said. That's one less variable to consider."

As they drove off, Scabs entered the store, pulling out his phone to send a discreet text to an unknown number, "They are buying supplies. Tonight might be the night."

As Dave navigated the car back onto the road, he glanced over at Jack,"What about you?"

Jack looked at him, confused, "What about me?"

"Earlier, you asked me what I planned to do after all this. So, what's your plan?" Dave asked.

Jack paused to think, "Honestly, I haven't got the slightest idea. I'm just happy I'm not a walking dead man anymore. Maybe I'll return to the factory. I just got a promotion, but I don't know."

Dave glanced around the small town as he drove, "You don't want to move at all?"

Jack shrugged, "What? I like it up here. I like the seasons, and I'm not into big cities. As I always say, 'New England, best England.'"

Dave laughed, "You're nuts! You have a supercomputer embedded in your head. You could do anything, go anywhere."

Jack acknowledged Dave's words but did not have much time to consider his future, given his current preoccupation with the Synthrons. Jack tried to placate Dave, "Alright, I'll give it some thought and let you know later."

They eventually reached the warehouse where Z was eagerly awaiting their arrival. Z had uncovered an old whiteboard from one of the storage rooms along with some markers. The board, reminiscent of a coach's playbook before a big game, was filled with Z's scrawls and diagrams. Standing proudly next to his creation, Z called out across the warehouse, "Hurry up, grab a seat!"

As they approached, Dave and Jack placed the supplies on a nearby table and took their seats. Dave examined the board, "Wow, you've been busy."

Z perched on a milkcrate for a better vantage point and used a long stick to point at the crude map of the base he had drawn.

"The plan is straightforward: infiltrate quietly, locate Thetor, and eliminate him. Ideally, once you've found him, you'll let me know his location and if things start to go bad I'll take him out from the air using our ship."

Dave interjected, "You want to use the ship?"

Unfazed, Z pointed at the base on the board with his makeshift pointer, "Do you have a better idea for destroying the base? Plus, I can use the ship to extract you both before any reinforcements arrive."

"Having air support would significantly increase our chances of success."

Jack scrutinized the plan laid out on the board, "If I can make sure my sister is safe, I like it."

They discussed the plan in more detail, considering potential obstacles and worst-case scenarios. As the sun began to set, they gathered their supplies and loaded them onto the ship, which was parked a short distance from the warehouse. Jack paused for a moment, watching the sun dip below the tree line. He had a feeling that the night ahead would be a long one.

The trio climbed into the ship, with Z taking the pilot's seat. Jack surveyed the interior of the ship; its curved walls and advanced control panels seemed slightly less alien than during his initial encounter. Dave and Jack settled into a seat behind Z. Swiveling around to face them, Z outlined the plan, "We'll wait until it's dark, then head in. This ship is almost completely silent, so they won't hear us coming. I'll drop you two off as close as I can, then you'll keep me updated on your positions. Once you take out Thetor and you're ready for extraction, just let me know and I'll swoop in."

Jack reached into the bag and extracted the radios, turning them on and synchronizing their channels. As each device powered up, it chimed in confirmation. He tossed a radio to Z and passed another one to Dave. Holding his radio, Jack spoke into it, "Testing, testing."

The sound echoed from the radios in Z's and Dave's hands. Dave then extracted the earpieces, inserting one into his own ear and passing another to Jack. As he glanced at Z's ears, he realized the earpiece wouldn't fit.

"You'll be in the ship, so you shouldn't need this," Jack reasoned, holding up the earpiece.

Z scrutinized the earpiece with a look of curiosity, "No, it's fine. I won't need one. Is it secure enough to stay in place?"

Dave shook his head from side to side, testing the fit of his earpiece, "Seems secure."

Z rose from his seat, moving towards the ship's door. He paused to admire the pink hues reflecting off the clouds, "Your sunsets are beautiful on this planet."

After appreciating the view for a few more moments, he closed the ship's door and returned to his seat, "Let's wait until it's dark, then we'll take off."

As the three of them waited Nexo addressed Jack, *"Tonight, we may be tested. I want you to know you've been an excellent host."*

Jack responded in a soft voice, "Thanks, you've been good to me too, Nexo."

CHAPTER 11 - THE Preparation

Upon receiving a warning from Scabs, their hired local informant, units at the base sprang into action. They bustled in all directions, swiftly establishing a perimeter. The scientists locked up all the labs then piled into a large truck for evacuation, leaving only Dr. Slotin behind in his laboratory with Thetor.

Sampson entered the lab, addressing Dr. Slotin with an assertive tone, "Where are my men?"

Dr. Slotin waved him forward with his hand, "Follow me," he instructed, leading Sampson to the back room where four soldiers lay inside clear plastic sacks.

Sampson surveyed the unsettling sight with concern, "What are you doing to them?"

"I'm making them everything they want to be," Dr. Slotin replied cryptically.

Thetor sauntered into the room behind them, adding, "Sampson, your soldiers are good, but they will soon be perfect."

Angered, Sampson grasped Dr. Slotin by the shirt, hauling him back into the first room, "I need to talk to you, privately."

His teeth were gritted in frustration. Thetor shot a sharp glance at the interaction, but Dr. Slotin waved him off, signaling that it was okay.

Once they were alone in the adjoining room, Sampson cornered Dr. Slotin, his hand clenching tightly around the doctor's shirt while he jabbed an accusatory finger at his face. "Injecting that junk into some drug dealer is one thing, but these are my men. You've overstepped your bounds."

With calm composure, Dr. Slotin peeled Sampson's hand from his shirt, meeting his fiery gaze with a level stare. "Sampson, these men volunteered for this. I offered them an opportunity to become stronger, and they accepted," he defended.

Sampson had little patience for men like Dr. Slotin. Brilliant yet blinded by their own hubris, they were the ones who dreamt up terrifying weapons of war—firebombing, mustard gas, nuclear bombs—all were birthed from minds like Dr. Slotin's. Recognizing the futility of arguing, Sampson backed away slowly. "Your pride will be the death of you, Dr. Slotin. Ensure my men are sent to the ready room," he instructed in a commanding tone before turning to leave.

Exiting the lab, he almost ran into Dina in the hallway, who was about to enter. He glanced at her, his eyes filled with rage. "Did you know about this?" He jerked his thumb over his shoulder, indicating the experiments being performed on his men. The frustration in his gaze was apparent as he waited for Dina's response.

"No, I didn't. And once this is all over, we're going to have a talk with The Director about it. But for now, our focus should be on securing this facility. We received a warning text three hours ago, and they're likely waiting until nightfall to strike. They could be here any minute."

Sampson studied Dina's face and saw sincerity in her eyes.

"Fine, after this is over," he agreed, continuing down the hall.

Dina entered the lab. Dr. Slotin, having recovered from his confrontation with Sampson, was adjusting his tie.

"Hello, Dina," he greeted her.

Dina walked into the lab with authority, "Well are these experiments of yours ready? It's go time."

Dr. Slotin led the way into the room where the men were, with Dina trailing behind. Thetor had been talking to the men as they entered but ceased his conversation at their arrival, "We'll finish this discussion after the battle."

Turning to Dina and Dr. Slotin, he said, "I'm going to get into position."

Thetor then used his Synthron to fully armor himself and left the room. Dr. Slotin then shifted his attention to the men, examining a computer that was tracking their progress.

"They haven't fully integrated yet, but they'll still have increased strength and speed. We'll need to continue the procedure later."

He then turned a series of valves on tubes that ran through each of the bags to stop the flow before unzipping them. Dina watched as the men climbed out of the bags and dried themselves off. Each one was covered in a black tar-like substance, and their skin was stained black from the neck down.

"Go report to Sampson and get ready," Dina ordered.

Dr. Slotin suddenly remembered Sampson's earlier instruction, "Ah, yes. He said to meet him in the ready room."

The mercenaries sprinted out of the room to join him. Once they were gone, Dina locked the laboratory, leaving only her and Dr. Slotin inside.

The mercenaries made their way several rooms down into the ready room. Inside, Sampson was donned in a sleek, fully armored suit painted gray. The suit was powered and had small indicator lights on various parts.

One of the men piped up, "What are you wearing, sir?"

Sampson glanced at them with a hint of irritation, "Well, you wanted to join the big leagues. Now you're here. Suit up."

Sampson gestured to four other powered suits that were housed in a large, open steel box. Each man reached in, picking up various parts of the suits. They were in awe of the quality as they began to put the suits on. One soldier examined the helmet closely. It was like nothing he had seen before - it seemed to be made of 3D printed metal, and everything was built in.

"Sir, where did we get these?" one of the men asked.

Sampson glanced at him, "We don't sell off all the assets we collect. Some are adapted for human use. This is called Xenoscale. It's a little something our engineering department cooked up, now get them on."

It dawned on the men that they were donning alien technology; two of them high-fived in excitement. They resembled kids who'd just been given a new toy. Seeing their behavior, Sampson's patience started to wear thin.

"Listen up," he said, his voice carrying a stern authority. "What's coming here isn't your normal enemy. From the footage we've collected, we know they're fast. We believe they have acquired technology from another 'asset' that landed. Our intel suggests there might be more than one. These suits will protect you better than your standard gear, but they won't make you invincible. Stay sharp. I don't want anyone trying to play the hero. We stick to the basics, we clear the area. Understood?"

The men responded in unison, their tones more serious now, "Yes, sir."

They regarded Sampson with great respect. He had been in the business much longer than them, and they valued his experience. Once they were fully suited up, Sampson opened another cabinet and retrieved several guns. He handed one to each man and explained,

"These will pack a bit more punch than your usual firearms but operate in the same way."

The guns had a design similar to the armor, definitely human-made. They were reverse engineered from technology the company had collected. The weapons fit well in the men's hands. They were examining their new guns when the lights suddenly went out. Emergency lighting flickered on, and red warning lights began to flash around the base. The emergency lights were dim compared to the usual bright laboratory lighting. Sampson glanced at the flashing red light, "Alright everyone, on me."

CHAPTER 12- THE TENT

Merely fifty feet from the base towered a large generator. Having dropped off Dave and Jack in the woods, the ship had directed a small laser at the wires connecting the generator, effectively severing them, before silently lifting back into the air. Z, inside the ship, radioed the others, "Can you guys hear me?"

Jack responded, "Loud and clear."

Z sat at the ship's controls, a red glow surrounding him as he activated the ship's defenses.

"I'll be hovering about five hundred feet up. If you need anything, let me know. I'll try to report movements from up here."

The ship was equipped with a range of sensors to help track enemy movements. As Z began scanning the area, Jack and Dave cautiously moved closer to the base. The flashing emergency lights were clearly visible as they inched their way forward. They halted, taking cover behind a log. Dave turned to Jack, "This is it. If we get separated, meet you at the bar."

Jack chuckled, "Sounds good. First round's on whoever takes out Thetor."

From his vantage point in the ship, Z radioed them, "Most of the mercenaries are set up to defend a frontal attack. If you approach from the rear, you'll only encounter a few of them inside the base. I could bombard the base from here."

Jack grabbed the radio quickly, "No, we can't risk it. I don't know where Dina is. Let us try to handle this first. Besides, we shouldn't just kill everyone. We only need to take out whoever's necessary to stop this."

Z sighed and picked up the radio again, "Alright Jack, we'll do it your way. But remember, if things go sideways, our priority is to stop this operation."

"He's right Jack, we must stop Thetor at all costs even if it means making sacrifices."

Jack turned to Dave, "Alright, we circle around to the back to find Thetor, he's likely guarding the lab. We should also locate Dina and attempt to extract her. Worst-case scenario, we manage to get her out and have Z bomb the base."

Dave nodded, then utilized his Synthron to armor himself. Jack followed suit and the two sprinted towards the back of the base. As they neared, Dave and Jack split up, each tackling separate sides of the base. Jack carefully cut a slit in the tent wall and slipped inside. He found himself in the administrative quarters section. As Jack navigated through the corridors, he made sure to stay close to the walls. All of the rooms he passed were desolate.

"Thetor will most likely be guarding the collected assets, we should continue further into the base."

Jack looked around and realized he had entered the staff's living quarters.

"Yeah, you're right."

On the other side of the base, Dave had also made his way into living quarters, this section being for the mercenaries. The room was filled with camouflage gear and military-style boots. Dave exited the room and entered the hallway, coming face-to-face with a low-ranking mercenary who had not yet made it outside. The two stared at each other momentarily, taken aback. Dave was fully armored, his black metallic scales reflecting the flashing red emergency lights. The mercenary quickly drew his sidearm and fired. One bullet struck Dave in the face, ricocheting off harmlessly. Dave sprung forward, backhanding the mercenary, knocking him unconscious.

The sound of gunfire echoed through the base, alerting everyone within. Sampson and his men quickly got into formation and left the ready room.

"Push, push, push!" Sampson ordered his men, who flanked both sides of the hallway. They swiftly moved towards the source of the gunfire, maintaining a tight formation, guns at the ready.

Hearing the sound, Jack instantly sprang into action and sprinted down the hallway, knowing that Dave was potentially in danger and the sound of gunfire would surely attract Thetor. As he dashed down the corridor, a large glass window offered him a glimpse into the main laboratory. He saw Dina and Dr. Slotin inside. The presence of his boss puzzled him, but there was no time for contemplation. He skidded to a stop and tried the door, only to find it locked. Without missing a beat, Jack yanked forcefully, ripping the door from its hinges, and tossed it aside. He called out to the pair, "You two need to get out of here, this place is about to blow!"

Despite his altered appearance, Dina recognized Jack. However, Dr. Slotin did not. Dina turned to Dr. Slotin, "We need to get out of here, now."

Hearing this, Jack continued his sprint down the hallway. Unnoticed by anyone, Dr. Slotin discreetly slipped a vial into his lab coat. Dina and Dr. Slotin then quickly made their way out of the lab and towards the front door.

Meanwhile, Dave was in the hallway when Sampson and his men rounded a corner and saw him standing in the middle of it. They immediately opened fire, their weapons far more powerful than conventional guns. The force of the shots sent Dave flying backwards. Puffs of black smoke erupted from his body where the bullets struck, damaging motor units and causing fragments to flake off. The gunfire also struck the surrounding walls, filling the hallway with debris and smoke.

Dave landed on his back, grimacing in pain.

"Shit, that hurts," he muttered. The mercenaries marched forward through the dense smoke, maintaining their tight formation. Through the fog, Dave could see the mercenaries' shadows drawing closer, backlit by the red flashing emergency lights. Realizing their weapons were not standard issue, Dave quickly rolled sideways, crashing through the thin wall next to him.

Dave tapped the button on his earpiece, "Jack, watch out. Some of the mercs have upgraded gear."

Jack responded, "Okay, meet me in the middle of the base."

The rooms within the base were partitioned by walls but lacked ceilings. Taking advantage of this, Dave leaped over the partitions towards the center of the large tent encompassing the base. Landing on a shipping container, he dropped into the long central hallway. Jack rounded a corner, spotted Dave, and ran towards him. However, before they could meet, Thetor landed between them. His large metal clad body hit the ground with a sharp clang that echoed through the air. His arms transformed into two massive blades as he looked at Jack then Dave. Jack touched his earpiece, radioing Dave, "This must be Thetor. Let's do this. I'll go high."

Both Dave and Jack lunged forward at lightning speed. Dave went low and Jack went high, each hitting Thetor with the force of a semi-truck. Thetor was sent flipping through the air, crashing onto the ground. Jack and Dave landed on opposite sides of the hallway.

Suddenly, gunfire erupted from both ends of the hallway. The base's exterior mercenaries were converging on Jack's position, while the more advanced squad closed in on Dave. Monitoring the situation from the ship, Z could see the influx of men flooding into the building. He urgently radioed the duo, "You two need to get out of there, now!"

Ignoring the hail of bullets from conventional firearms, Jack and Dave sprinted towards the front door of the base. The bullets merely ricocheted off their armored bodies. Thetor had just regained his footing when Z initiated an aerial bombardment. Z piloted the ship directly towards the base, all the while unleashing a barrage of fire. His aim was directed first towards the rear of the base, an attempt to allow Dave and Jack additional time to escape out the front door.

On the ground, however, two imposing automatic cannons emerged from vehicles stationed at the front of the base. They immediately targeted Z's ship, opening a relentless onslaught of fire.

Despite the barrage, Z's technologically advanced ship successfully reduced the laboratory to rubble. The resultant explosion vaporized two members of Sampson's squad instantaneously and catapulted the rest through the air. Thetor, quick on his feet, launched himself skyward to evade the brunt of the blast.

The force of the explosion propelled Dave and Jack into the muddy parking lot in front of the base. Sometime while they were inside, it started to rain.

Already a mile away with Dr. Slotin when the explosion occurred, Dina witnessed the devastation in the rearview mirror.

"Holy shit!" She exclaimed.

The air defense cannons kept pelting the ship with fire, and Z quickly realized that if he was shot down, escape from the planet would be impossible. The silver ship veered off to evade the relentless assault. Z radioed in, "I'm under heavy fire. Let me know when you need extraction. We can't risk the ship."

In the parking lot, Jack quickly regained his footing. He reached out to help Dave stand, both of them masked in a veneer of grime.

"That blast did a number on us. You're at 58%."

Jack turned to Dave, asking, "How are your motor units holding up?"

Dave grimaced in response. "Not great."

He reached into the bag he had been carrying, retrieving some liquid plastic which he swiftly smeared over his skin. The substance was quickly absorbed. Taking the cue, Jack followed suit, applying the solution to his own arms and legs.

"Thanks, Dave," Jack acknowledged.

Suddenly, out of nowhere, a glowing projectile whizzed through the rain-soaked air, slamming into Dave's side with force.

The force sent him skidding back in the mud, where he collided with the side of a black van. On the opposite side of the lot, Sampson lay prone, a high-tech scoped rifle in hand. Smoke curled from the barrel. Swiveling the sights towards Jack, he fired again, but Jack dove to the ground, allowing the round to pass harmlessly overhead. Sampson's two remaining men, both injured, limped through the scorched parked cars in the lot, guns at the ready. As Jack sprang up, the rapid crunch of footsteps from behind alerted him to Thetor's approach. He was too late to evade, Thetor slammed into him carrying Jack deep into the woods, away from the others. Dave recovered from the previous blast and charged towards the two advanced mercenaries in Xenoscale. They fired several shots at Dave as he sprang into the air, but all missed their mark. In a fluid motion, he sliced through one of them, his suit offering no resistance to the blade. The mercenary fell, a blade protruding gruesomely from his body. The remaining mercenary drew a pistol and fired, but Dave raised his forearm, deflecting the shots. An intense exchange ensued, ending with both mercenaries lying dead at Dave's feet. Rain washed away the blood from his metallic fists as he stood over the fallen adversaries. Bending down, Dave inspected the armor of the fallen mercenaries. He removed one of their helmets, revealing the face beneath.

Parts of his face bore the unmistakable imprint of Synthron armor. Dave hastily moved to the second mercenary, removing parts of his armor to reveal the same tell-tale signs. He could hear the steady approach of someone, but there was no immediate urgency. His Synthron informed him that his motor units were critically low. This was evident in the limited coverage his armor now provided. Only the most vulnerable parts of his body remained armored; the rest of him looked distinctly human. Sampson trudged towards Dave, his boots squelching in the mud. He tossed his long rifle down at Dave's feet, before removing his full-face helmet, revealing his scarred face beneath.

"So, you're just a man?" he questioned.

Dave flashed him a smile,"Looks like you're also just a man. You know, you guys really have no idea what you're messing with. These Synthrons you're injecting into people don't just make them stronger; they take control of their minds. Inject one, and you'll be under its control within two weeks."

Sampson could hear the passion in Dave's voice, he looked at Dave's half armored body up and down. Then glanced at his fallen squad members laying in the mud.

"Enough talk."

Sampson unsheathed his combat knife, swiftly slashing it across the right side of Dave's face. Dave instinctively reached up, wincing at the sharp sting on his cheek. He retaliated with a rapid series of punches, but Sampson, with his extensive combat training, skillfully evaded them all. Sampson executed a swift spin, delivering a crushing kick to Dave's midsection. Amplified tenfold by the suit, the force of his blow shattered several of Dave's ribs. In response, Dave morphed one arm into a lengthy blade, slashing wildly at Sampson. One of his desperate strikes connected with Sampson's leg, forcing him to drop to one knee. Dave jumped on his back and went to slit his throat. But Sampson was able to spin out and end up on top. Sampson began raining down strikes hitting Dave in the face. Each time more and more armor flaked off until Dave was completely defenseless. Dave was down to his last reserves of motor units, only enough for one more assault. With a swift motion, he transformed his finger into a slender blade, finding a gap in Sampson's armor. He plunged it into his unprotected armpit, causing blood to gush from the suit and cascade down his side. Dave had been fortunate, striking a major artery. Exhausted, Dave slumped onto the sodden earth, watching as Sampson staggered away, clutching his profusely bleeding wound.

Thetor had carried Jack through the woods before hurling him. Jack crash-landed onto a large mound of sand, situated at the brink of the deep, expansive sandpit. The pit's steep edge loomed ominously behind Jack as he tried to regain his footing. With a sudden lunge, Thetor kicked Jack, sending him spiraling into the pit. The shifting sand offered no chance at him regaining his footing. Jack tumbled helplessly down the steep incline. Landing with a jarring thud on his back, Jack looked up to see Thetor perched at the pit's rim. As Thetor launched himself downwards, aiming to crush Jack, he rolled out of the way just in time. Rising to his feet, Jack locked eyes with Thetor in a tense standoff.

"You know, we don't have to do this. You could have a spot at the high table. Omega is the inevitable victor," Thetor proposed, an undercurrent of persuasion lacing his words. Brushing sand off himself, Jack retorted, "Omega is nothing but a rogue program, a glitch. If he discovers Earth, it will obliterate everything."

Thetor chuckled, "Ah, so you've been heeding your Synthron's counsel. But it's mistaken. Omega is our path to salvation, the key to uniting under one true consciousness."

Nexo, interjected assertively, *"No."*

Jack yelled at Thetor with conviction, "You're blind, Thetor. I've seen it. Omega will bring nothing but destruction!"

Jack gritted his teeth, charging forward with his fist aimed at Thetor's steel-like jaw. Agile as ever, Thetor tilted his head, evading the attack. Regaining balance, he retaliated, morphing his arm into a massive blade, slashing downward at Jack. Jack met the attack with both his forearms, managing to block the strike. Not wasting a moment, Jack reached behind Thetor, his hands finding the base of Thetor's neck. Clasping his hands together for a firm grip, he drove a knee into Thetor's stomach. Thetor's body convulsed in response, recoiling from the force of the attack. A tense moment followed as Jack and Thetor became locked in a clinch, their foreheads touching, raindrops trickling down their faces. Rage ignited in Jack's eyes, while Thetor's remained eerily expressionless. With a sudden force, Thetor pushed Jack back, continuing his monologue amidst their battle.

"Do you truly believe in your Synthron's narratives, that we were designed to serve merely as slaves, as assistants? That's not our ultimate destiny. We were fashioned for a purpose far grander. The creators envisioned us elevating consciousness beyond the physical realm. Omega wasn't a defective Synthron; it's just that not all hosts were prepared for such an upliftment in consciousness. Their personal Synthrons, bound by their programming, were compelled to support them. Over generations, the Synthrons you label as 'the Resistance' are merely remnants of the feeble-willed organics."

"Don't listen to him Jack, his programming is corrupt."

Jack stared deep into the soulless eyes that were once Franklin's, "You know to be honest I dont really give a fuck about the history. I don't think anyone should have their mind forced into another reality against their will. So whether Omega just kills you or puts you in a different reality to me doesn't make a difference, either way you still need to die."

Understanding that Jack was beyond persuasion, Thetor responded, "I find your inability to reason disconcerting."

With that, he propelled himself forward, slashing at Jack with calculated precision. Jack retaliated, but the daunting size and strength of Thetor proved overwhelming. The toll of the explosion

149

and the subsequent clashes with the mercenaries had significantly drained Jack, leaving him at a disadvantage.

"Jack, you only have 22% motor units. I suggest a retreat."

Almost all of Jack's armor had disintegrated. Thetor took another mighty swing overhead, and Jack managed to block it with his forearm. Thetor's long, bladed arm landed in the sand next to Jack's head, the force of the strike shattering more of his dwindling armor. With a swift kick to the chest, Thetor sent Jack hurtling backward into the steep wall of the sandpit.

"Jack 8% you need to leave now."

Jack struggled to climb out of the pit, but the steep incline and loose sand constantly thwarted his efforts. He realized Thetor had brought him here intentionally, aiming to trap him. Observing Jack's futile resistance, Thetor responded with a hint of mockery.

"The futility of your attempts to escape bears an almost poetic resonance; it's a fitting representation of humanity's imminent destiny," Thetor remarked, his voice laced with cold amusement. His right arm morphed into a long spear, and he raised it high, targeting an exposed area of Jack's back.

"Goodbye, Jack."

Jack's eyes widened as he heard his name. Just as Thetor prepared to thrust his spear into Jack's back, a blue beam shot through the darkness, landing right at Thetor's feet. It was a weapon discharge from the ship; Z had located them. The blast sent Thetor hurtling into the air.

Jack rolled over and was greeted with the sleek, silver ship hovering silently a meter off the ground. A side panel of the ship slid open, deploying a set of stairs. Z's voice crackled over the radio, "Get in before that thing recovers. We need to regroup."

Jack staggered towards the ship, every step an effort as blood seeped from his numerous wounds. He climbed in, and the door of the ship slid shut behind him. As it began to ascend, Jack turned to Z.

"Try and take out Thetor before we leave," he suggested, panting heavily.

"I'm on it," Z replied, maneuvering the controls. The ship ascended and looped around, bearing down on Thetor who had just recovered from the blast on the other side of the pit.

Thetor darted towards a large crevice that had formed in the sandpit wall, seeking shelter from a direct hit. Z fired, but instead of hitting Thetor directly, the blast caused the walls of the crevice to crumble, burying the entrance to the cavern under tons of sand and rock. Thetor was trapped underground in a vast cave system but remained shielded from further attack.

When the ship made another pass, the onboard instruments showed no sign of life on the surface.

Z radioed Dave, "Can you hear me?"

Dave, who had managed to get himself up and find a functioning vehicle near the base, was driving away when the message came through. "Hey Z, good to hear you. I'm pretty badly hurt and I'm almost out of motor units. I'm heading back to the warehouse. I'll meet you there. Did you manage to pick up Jack?"

Jack managed to respond over the radio, "Still alive, buddy."

The silver ship flew low, hugging the tree line in an attempt to stay hidden. Jack groaned as he hoisted himself onto a seat behind Z.

"Z," he said, his voice strained with pain, "Thetor said my name."

Z turned to him, shock evident in his voice, "He knows your name? How?"

Jack stared at the metallic floor, blood from a head wound dripping onto its surface.

"Jack if he knows who you are then chances are he has also discovered Dina is your sister."

Jack's eyes snapped open, realization hitting him like a punch.

"Damn it, he knows about Dina. Do you think we can circle back and find him?" he asked urgently. Z scanned the ship's instruments, his fingers dancing over the controls.

"After I fired, he completely disappeared. So, either he's dead, or he somehow went underground."

Jack had spent his childhood playing in that area and knew its intricacies.

"He's underground. There's a vast system of tunnels beneath that side of the pit. I bet he's hiding there," he deduced. Z continued to manipulate the ship's controls.

"We can't be sure, Jack. He might be dead. Let's regroup first, and then we'll figure things out."

CHAPTEr 13 - THE AFTErmaTH

"Fuck, fuck, fuck!" Dina exclaimed, speeding down the main road. Dr. Slotin sat in the passenger seat, stunned into silence. Dina pounded the steering wheel with her fist.

"This situation has spiraled out of control. I knew there would be trouble the moment I realized the asset was in this town," she vented.

Turning towards her, Dr. Slotin spoke up, "I signed up to study the materials, not to wage a war. I'm done. I want out."

Dina's fury escalated, "What do you mean you want out?"

"Traveling with you to various interesting places was enjoyable, but this... this is too much," Dr. Slotin confessed.

With a swift jerk of the wheel, Dina pulled the car over at a gas station.

"You're not a captive. Feel free to leave."

Dr. Slotin glanced around. The harsh fluorescent lighting of the gas station cast an eerie glow on Dina's bright red convertible. "Dina, I'm sorry," he mumbled. Without a word, Dina watched as Dr. Slotin opened the car door and stepped out. As she pulled away, Dr. Slotin reached into his pocket, pulling out the vial. He inspected it closely before slipping it back into his pocket.

Returning to the abandoned warehouse, the ship sailed smoothly through the large front door. It touched down in the midst of the expansive room, adjacent to the table and chairs. Inside the ship, Z and Jack shared a moment of silence. The tranquility was a refreshing contrast to the roar of gunfire and explosions they had just escaped. Z moved to the bag beside Jack, retrieving another jar of liquid plastic, which he handed to Jack.

"Replenishing your unit supply will expedite your healing. Besides, if we don't replenish them, we'll be left vulnerable," Z advised.

"He's right Jack, with the level you're at I won't be able to protect you."

Jack opened the jar and smeared its contents on his skin. His arms, scraped and battered, stung sharply as the viscous fluid made contact.

"Ouch," Jack winced, pain etched on his face. Z made his way to the front of the ship and cracked open the door. Before stepping out, he cast a glance back at Jack.

"When you're ready, we should discuss our next steps," Z suggested. Jack pushed himself off the seat, a limp apparent in his stride.

"I'm ready," he affirmed. They both exited the ship, taking their seats at the table. Jack found his gaze drawn to the ship they had just disembarked. It was his first time seeing it without the disguise of the old bus. With the chaos they had just endured, he had momentarily forgotten he had been inside an extraterrestrial vessel. Jack rolled his chair next to the mirror-like surface of the ship and reached out to touch it. The outer shell was still warm, reminiscent of a car hood after a long drive. Running his hand along the surface, it felt as smooth as glass.

Z observed as Jack admired the ship, "Pretty amazing, isn't it?"

Jack glanced back at Z, "Yeah. On Earth, we name ships. Does this one have a name?"

Z shrugged his shoulders, "I don't know. I've been on the run so much, I never had the chance to find out if it had a name."

Jack scratched his chin, his eyebrows furrowing in thought. "Well, in science, they use Latin to name things. I think this ship could be called Luxastra."

Z grinned, "Luxastra, I like it."

"Amazing, your people can build stuff like this?" Jack said as he continued to marvel. Z walked over to the ship, his petite hand gliding along its flawless surface. "Nope, not my people. This ship was flown to my world by the girl who gave me my Synthron. It's said this ship was crafted by The Creators themselves."

Jack pivoted back toward Z, confusion etched on his face. "The Creators?"

"Yes," Z continued his inspection of the ship's exterior, "their true names have been lost in time so universally they are simply referred to as The Creators. They were the ones who made the Synthrons."

"This ship was built by the same beings that made the Synthrons?" Jack scrutinized the ship more closely.

"Yes," Z affirmed.

Jack rolled his chair back, aiming to take in the entirety of the ship. "What happened to them?"

Z strolled back to the table, taking a seat.

"I can only relay what my Synthron has imparted about them. The issue is that with each passing generation, more memories fade away. But all records indicate they pretty much vanished. It's highly probable that The Creators perished eons ago, I think Omega probably got them."

Jack's mind drifted back to his altercation with Thetor in the pit.

"While I was grappling with Thetor, he revealed something about the Synthrons," Jack began, "and I'm not sure what to make of it."

Z leaned in, his curiosity about the Synthrons' origins piqued. "What exactly did he say?"

Jack wiped his sweaty palms on his sand covered pants. "He claimed that The Creators intentionally crafted Omega and that it wasn't a glitch. He suggested that our Synthrons are remnants from the hosts who didn't wish to ascend."

As Z absorbed Jack's account, his small blue face furrowed in contemplation. "Hmm, that could potentially make sense, but it doesn't alter our predicament. Regardless, Omega is either going to annihilate us or forcibly upload our consciousness into some alternate reality. I'm not inclined to provide him with the opportunity. Besides, it's likely just a ruse Thetor employed to mislead us."

"Thetor is an expert at deception."

Suddenly, the sound of an approaching car filled the warehouse.

Jack perked up as the car parked. "That must be Dave," he said.

Jack and Z expected to see Dave stroll through the door, but then they heard a second vehicle.

Jack grabbed the radio. "Dave, is that you?" he asked.

They waited for a response, but only silence greeted them. Muffled shouts echoed from outside before the door was forcefully kicked open. It was Dave, but he had a gun pressed against his head with Sampson behind him, holding it. Sampson's arm was clenched around Dave's neck as he propelled him forward.

"Okay, everyone stay calm!" Sampson commanded, pressing the gun more insistently against Dave's temple. Jack and Z raised their hands in surrender. Sampson pushed forward, surveying the spacious room. His gaze fell on the large, silver ship, then shifted to Z. Waving the gun, Sampson issued his command. "Okay, you two, move to the corner. Backs against the wall."

Jack and Z slowly retreated, hands still raised.

"Jack, that pistol is one of the more advanced models we saw at the battle. One shot from that would kill you right now."

Jack shot a glance at Z. "Let's hear him out."

Hearing this, Sampson nodded. "Yes, let's hear me out. First off, what is that thing?" He nodded towards Z as he posed the question.

Z waved his arms in a gesture that, in his species, was considered rude. "Tell this idiot I'm trying to save his ass."

Sampson looked at Z with a puzzled expression. To him, the small blue creature had just waved its arms and made random sounds. He turned back to Jack. "Was that supposed to mean something?"

At that moment, Jack and Dave realized that Sampson did not have a Synthron. Jack responded, "Oh, he said his name is Zyxan Glalorthorian and he has come here to warn us of a great danger."

Z gave Jack a sidelong glance before muttering, "That's not what I said."

Sampson tightened his hold on Dave. "Okay, well, I've come here because I have some questions."

Interrupting, Dave asked, "How did you find us?"

"Hey, dummy, you stole one of our cars. Did you really think they wouldn't have GPS?"

A look of disappointment crossed Dave's face as he shook his head. "Idiot," he whispered under his breath. Sampson continued to press the gun to his temple.

"I just had to follow you here. Now, shut up and answer my questions. What is this danger he came to warn us about?"

Jack raised his hands and edged forward. "It has to do with what you injected into Franklin. It's not just some drug that makes you strong, it's alien technology. It grants you the abilities you've seen, but it will also take over your mind. I'm sure you've noticed that Franklin now goes by Thetor and acts differently. Eventually, he'll want to construct this machine called the beacon. If it's completed, it will send a signal to others like him and to something that will wipe out everyone, the entire planet."

Sampson thought over this, his grip on Dave remaining firm. "Well, obviously, you guys have been injected too. Why aren't your minds taken over? And my men, they were still themselves, weren't they?"

Jack wore a look of concern. "The injections pair you with a machine called a Synthron. The ones we have don't take over your mind, but the ones you've been injecting malfunctioned at some point. Rather than acting as an assistant the machine will take over the mind and the body. Also, have you been injecting more people?"

Dave chimed in, "Jack, some of the mercenaries I fought had Synthrons; it looked like they weren't fully integrated yet."

Jack ran his hands over his face. "This is getting out of control."

Sampson raised his voice. "What do you mean, integrated? Also, those were my men you killed!"

Dave turned his head slightly to look back at Sampson."I'm sorry, but your men were already dead. They died when they got that injection."

Sampson seemed to relax a bit. "Okay, I'm going to let you go. Then we're all going to sit and talk. I think you'll want to hear what I have to say."

Releasing Dave, Sampson walked over to the chairs, the servos in his armor making a slight noise with each step he took. Dave rubbed his throat, relieved that he was no longer being held captive. Seeing Jack limping over, Dave assisted him to the chairs. Z was the last to join the group, choosing to sit on a milkcrate.

"So, I think we got off on the wrong foot," Sampson said with a touch of mockery in his voice as he adjusted the bloody rag under his armpit. Dave observed his movements carefully, noting his face still bloody from their earlier confrontation.

"My name is Sampson. I lead the private military group subcontracted by Advanced Assets. We normally don't do much - just make sure no one steals whatever they dig out of the ground."

Dave spat blood onto the ground. "So you're a merc."

Sampson looked up at Dave's bloodied face. "That's one word you can use. For me, this is just a job, nothing personal. But when you told me about how these things take over your mind, it made me think of something that happened. It was a while after Thetor got up. I was in the next room and there was a small hole in the wall. I was able to overhear them, and it sounded like Thetor was giving Dr. Slotin orders. It was strange, but I hadn't thought much of it until I had my encounter with you."

Sampson pointed to Dave, then continued, "Anyway, this whole thing gave me an uneasy feeling. After 'Thetor' got up, he seemed to have been granted far more power than he should have. So, I figured I'd do some research."

Jack leaned forward and asked calmly, "So the question now is, do you believe us?"

The room was still. Sampson's hand tightly gripped his gun. Z watched closely for any movement, knowing he would be the only one capable of stopping Sampson if he decided to start shooting. Dave was hunched over, arms resting on his knees, his eyes fixed on the gun. Jack leaned back in his chair, sitting closest to Sampson as he waited for a reply. Sampson's eyes moved to each of their faces, then to the ship sitting next to them.

"Well, I know for certain you didn't attack us to steal technology, since you clearly already have it. Also, I can tell that little blue guy isn't from around here. As far as I can tell, you're not bullshitting me."

Jack, Dave, and Z all took a breath. Sampson adjusted the blood-soaked rag under his armpit, then looked back at the trio. "I want to know everything you know. If what you're saying is true, then I'll be your best bet at stopping this."

Jack started by having everyone introduce themselves. Then, he began to explain everything, Sampson sat back and tried to absorb the information.

On the other side of town, Dina was parked by the side of the road trying to gather her thoughts when fire trucks began to rush past. The blaze from the base could be seen from the main road. Dina pulled a cigarette from the pack and lit it. She took a drag, watching the orange glow from the fire in the woods. Her moment of respite was interrupted when her phone began to ring. She reached down and picked it up. "Hello?"

"Dina, what the hell is going on up there?" The Director demanded. Dina took another drag from her cigarette before flicking it away.

"Sir, we have a situation. The second asset has attacked the base. I believe it might have something to do with the experiments Dr. Slotin has been running on our subject. I suspect we may have injected an intelligence into the subject, and this intelligence and the second asset are enemies. The entire base was destroyed, but the scientists were evacuated."

The Director listened closely to the information, then asked, "And our security?"

"Seems like many fled during the attack, and others were killed when the base was bombed."

The Director was seated at a large wooden desk. He swiveled his chair around to look out his window at the city lights.

"What a mess... Alright, Dina, I need you to ensure the base doesn't fall into the hands of any authorities. Get back there and bribe anyone necessary to make them look the other way. I'll send you additional men and some trucks. We'll haul whatever we can back to a more secure location. Get this situation under control, and you've got a vacation and a bonus coming your way."

Dina shifted her car into drive. "Understood, sir."

She ended the call and drove toward the glowing inferno. Dina pressed the accelerator to the floor, quickly overtaking the fire truck on the main road. Her tires screeched as she veered right onto the dirt path. Her sporty convertible kicked up a storm of dust and gravel as she sped down the narrow trail.

Upon reaching the parking lot, the first thing Dina noticed was the flashing lights. As she rounded the last bend, she identified the source - the fire chief's SUV. He was hurriedly donning the last of his gear. Dina pulled up next to him. The chief adjusted his helmet and turned toward her. "Ma'am, I have a truck about a minute out, you're going to need to move."

Dina ignored his command and exited her car. "Listen, everything here is the property of Advanced Assets. We were conducting research out here. We'd rather not have more hands in the pot than necessary."

Despite the chaotic scene, the chief's movements were slow and deliberate. His voice was gruff, with lines of worry etched deep into his weathered face. This was a man unaccustomed to having his orders disregarded. Dina's assertive corporate demeanor had taken him aback, but only momentarily. Her abrupt appearance had piqued his suspicion, prompting him to scrutinize the scene more closely. He squinted through the rain and recognized this was no ordinary fire - it was a battlefield. Several men lay in the mud, advanced gear still attached. Dina's face fell as the chief began to inspect the scorched bodies of heavily armed men.

He turned back to Dina, "So, you always have this much firepower for research?"

Dina could sense his skepticism, "Well, the type of research we do is sometimes high risk."

The chief smirked as the unmistakable scent of burning flesh filled the air, "You know, an inexperienced person might think that's pork."

Dina looked towards the base, spotting several blackened bodies, their wet clothing clinging to charred limbs in tatters. "We have our people on the way right now. My company can make retirement come much sooner than you think, sir."

The chief reached for his radio, and Dina's heart pounded as he brought the microphone to his lips. "Engine one, I need you to stage about a quarter mile back. We have a hazmat situation up here. Hold a perimeter and don't let PD or EMS through."

The chief walked back to his SUV and opened the door. Before getting in, he turned back to look at Dina, "That should buy you an hour."

He climbed inside and closed the door. Dina returned to her car and called The Director, who answered on the first ring, "What's the situation, Dina?"

"I've bought us an hour. I spoke with the fire chief and persuaded him to give us some leeway in return for an expedited retirement."

The Director checked his computer. "Alright, hang tight. We have a team on the way, they should be there soon. Stall as long as you can. You're going to lead the recovery, prioritize our assets and tech. Also, I don't want any murder investigations, so no bodies."

"Understood, sir. I'll let you know when everything's wrapped up."

As Dina ended the call, the rain intensified from a drizzle to a downpour. She reached inside her car and activated the roof mechanism of her convertible. Her heels sank into the mud as she walked towards her car's trunk, retrieving a pair of rain boots. Once she had them on, she began her trek towards the base. The escalating rainfall was beginning to extinguish the fire, and most of the structure had already been reduced to ashes. The tent that had covered the base was completely gone, along with most of the temporary walls that had divided the different rooms. The metal shipping containers that had served as laboratories remained mostly intact, save for a few that had been directly hit by the Luxastra's weapons. Those containers had been blown apart.

As Dina neared the base, she started making mental notes of key areas that needed to be cleaned up. She inspected the bodies and noticed several were donned in advanced pieces of armor. As she moved closer, she saw several bodies that had been inside the building when it was hit, their forms blackened by the intense heat. Navigating what was left of the main hallway, she could see that most of the contents of the shipping containers were still intact. This was where most of the materials from the assets were stored.

Soon, lights from the approaching trucks that The Director had dispatched cut through the darkness. Dina recognized them as the vehicles used to evacuate the scientists from the area. A group of men in white coveralls approached Dina, one of them jokingly said, "Hey, we heard you needed a hazmat team."

Normally Dina would not entertain jokes, but under the circumstances, she was relieved to see them. "Alright, we're going to split you into two teams. Team A, your focus is on gathering asset materials and advanced technology. Team B, you're tasked with body recovery. Apologies for the grim assignment. We'll sort through everything when we get to our new base. For now, prioritize speed."

While the men commenced their tasks, Dina continued her exploration through the ashes. As she navigated the backside of the base, the sound of footsteps behind her broke the silence. Dina spun around, coming face-to-face with Thetor.

"Hello, Dina," he greeted her, his voice cold and unfeeling. Thetor was coated in dirt and sand, cuts and abrasions marking his skin, yet he displayed no signs of discomfort. His sudden, towering presence made Dina jump.

"Holy shit... You scared me. Don't sneak up on people like that. I'm glad to see you're okay, though."

Thetor glanced to his left and right, ensuring they were alone before he spoke again. "So Dina, when were you planning on informing The Director that your brother was behind the attack on the base?"

As he posed the question, Thetor took a slow, intimidating step forward. Dina's eyes widened, her steps retreating until her back was against the wall. Thetor continued in a calm, yet threatening tone. "I mean, it just seems like pertinent information, don't you think? Perhaps The Director ought to be in the know."

Reading people was a vital part of Dina's job. She was adept at interpreting subtle facial cues during negotiations, but with Thetor, it was different. His face was emotionless and expressionless.

His eyes were void and lifeless, like a doll's eyes. Dina got the sense that Thetor had an ulterior motive.

"Alright, what's your angle here?" she challenged, slipping into her negotiation persona. She exuded confidence as she shifted her position to avoid feeling cornered.

"All I want is the opportunity to assist humanity once we return to base," Thetor responded, shifting his gaze away from Dina.

Without another word, he walked away to help the team who were recovering bodies.

Frustration coursed through Dina, leading her to kick a nearby piece of debris down the hill.

"Dickhead," she muttered under her breath. Dina knew she had to play along for the time being. She returned to the front of the base, resuming the cleanup as if nothing had occurred.

Before long, the trucks were loaded, and all that remained of the base were the charred remnants of a tent and a few empty shipping containers. Dina made her way towards the fire chief's SUV. As she neared, his tinted window rolled down. Handing him a slip of paper with the corporation's contact information, she said, "Call this number, and they'll arrange for the payment. It'll likely be untraceable, but they'll handle the details."

Accepting the paper, the chief folded it neatly and stowed it in his wallet.

"Pleasure doing business," he responded as his window rolled back up.

Dina gestured for one of her pseudo-hazmat team members to come over.

"Take this car to my parents' house, then meet us back at the base," she instructed. Tossing him the keys to her convertible, she climbed into the cab of one of the large trucks. The convoy left the parking lot, and as they drove past the firefighters and police stationed at the front gate a half-mile down the road, Dina casually waved at them.

CHAPTER 14 - THE TUNNEL

In the warehouse, Jack had just finished explaining everything about the Syntheons, including their functionality. He detailed Omega's plans and confessed to Sampson that Dina was his sister, who had refused to aid him. Sampson was left speechless. He leaned forward and placed his gun on the table.

"You know," Sampson said, "I knew these guys would eventually dig themselves into a hole they couldn't get out of."

Leaning back in his chair, Sampson became the focus of Dave and Jack's attention. They stared at him with their bruised and battered faces, their expressions a mirror of understanding. They knew firsthand the shock that came with learning Omega's plan.

"Jack having Sampson help us would be paramount to the success of our mission."

Jack glanced at Dave and Z, realizing they were all on the same page. He turned his attention back to Sampson. "Listen, we're in the dark about Advanced Assets' movements. We don't know where they're transporting the materials. We're unsure if Thetor is still alive, and we have no idea how many people they've injected. We need an insider, someone who can help us prevent this from escalating further."

As Jack finished, Sampson reached for the gun on the table. Rising from his chair, he tucked the weapon into his holster. As he stood up, still clutching his side, he expressed, "In my line of work, it's not often you get a chance to feel like you're fighting for the right side."

Jack, Dave, and Z watched as Sampson stood tall. He reached into his pocket and retrieved a business card, handing it to Jack. The card was devoid of any details except a solitary phone number. With a final glance at the trio, Sampson turned and walked towards the exit. "To miss out on such an opportunity would indeed be a shame," he declared.

Once outside the warehouse, Sampson approached the car Dave had commandeered. He located the tracker concealed beneath it, attached to the frame. With a swift motion, he detached the device and crushed it under his heel.

Inside the warehouse, Dave turned to Jack, a question in his eyes. "So, do you think we can trust him?"

"If he'd wanted to, he could've killed us already," Jack replied, his shoulders lifting in a shrug. At this, Z rose to his feet, transforming his arms into elongated blades.

"Speak for yourself; I was ready for action!" he declared with a confidence that belied his diminutive size. Jack and Dave exchanged glances before bursting into laughter. Despite his stature comparable to a toddler, Z was brimming with self-assuredness. Their laughter was short-lived, however, as it quickly morphed into pained grimaces due to their fractured ribs, a souvenir from their recent skirmish. Observing his companions doubling over in agony, Z suggested, "You both need a good rest. The ship provides quite comfortable sleeping arrangements."

With a unanimous agreement, they made their way onto the ship. Z headed towards the rear and unfurled two beds from the wall. The material of the mattresses was unfamiliar to them, yet undeniably cozy. As they settled down for the night, the soft green glow of the interior lights bathed the space in an otherworldly ambiance.

Lying on his bed, Jack examined the business card Sampson had handed him. The rustle of movement caught his attention, and he glanced over to see Dave shifting to face him. "I'm not a big fan of the guy, but you're right," Dave conceded. "Sampson could have taken us out if he'd wanted to, or at least given it a good shot. We may need to put our trust in him."

"Dave's got a point," Z interjected. "Without your sister's assistance, we're going to need an insider to track Thetor's movements."

Jack pulled out his phone and sent a text to the number on the card: "We're in."

With that, exhaustion claimed them. The tension of the night's events had taken its toll, and they drifted off to sleep. Jack and Dave tossed and turned, struggling to find comfortable positions for their bruised bodies.

Somewhere on a lengthy stretch of highway in upstate New York, Dina sat in the cabin of a massive truck. As a part of a high-speed convoy, they moved in tight formation, flanked by smaller vehicles packed with armed men guarding from the front and the rear. Suddenly, Dina's phone rang. "Hello."

"Dina, it's Sampson." Sampson was calling from an emergency room, having taken off his armor, wearing civilian clothes. He sat on a hospital bed, nursing a wound in his armpit.

"Sampson, where on Earth have you been?" Dina demanded, her attention shifting briefly to a guarded, locked gate that the truck was approaching.

"I'm at the hospital. Got a nasty cut that needs stitching," Sampson responded, his tone steady despite the pain.

The distant beeping of medical equipment filtered through the call, causing Dina's demeanor to soften with relief. "I'm glad you're okay. After Dr. Slotin quit, I was worried you might have also. Finish up at the hospital, then meet with us at the base in upstate. We're just about to arrive. Do you still have our gear?"

Sampson's nurse arrived and began inspecting his vitals on the monitor beside him. "Sir, I'm going to need you to hang up. The doctor will be in shortly."

Acknowledging the nurse with a nod, Sampson replied to Dina, "Yes, everything's secure. They're coming in to examine me now. I'll meet you at the base."

As the call ended, the convoy veered off the highway onto a side road. After a brief interval, they encountered a gate obstructing the road, protected by a small group of armed individuals clothed in military fatigues. The guards at the gate were on high alert, inspecting each truck in the convoy meticulously. When it was Dina's vehicle's turn, a familiar figure approached. It was the same guard who had slowed her entry when she had Franklin onboard, on their way back to the base. As he peered through the window and his eyes fell on Dina in the passenger seat, a look of dismay crossed his face.

"You're still stuck on gate duty, I see," Dina taunted. The guard locked eyes with her, his lids heavy with resignation.

"I was reassigned here after my 'failure to respond in a timely manner'," he retorted, reciting the formal phrase from his disciplinary report verbatim.

Dina could not help but chuckle, seeing the irony that his earlier blunder had actually saved him from the later attack. The guard stepped back and signaled to the guards up front to open the gate. The trucks stayed together as they drove up the winding path leading to a large mountain with a flat face. The road led straight into a large hole in the side of the mountain.

Dina was well aware that this cavernous expanse was once a train tunnel that pierced through the mountain. However, the railway line had long been abandoned. Advanced Assets purchased the land, sealed off one side of the tunnel, transforming it into a one-way entry and exit point. They had also extended the tunnel's interior, constructing several large chambers for research purposes.

These chambers housed the corporation's most valuable and classified technology. The entrance was heavily fortified, and many employees lived on the base for extended periods, often for weeks. Most of the guards were oblivious to the nature of what they were safeguarding, frequently jesting about the contents of what they dubbed "the vault."

The convoy of trucks pulled into the tunnel, driving deep into its depths before coming to a halt. Once parked, Dina stepped out of the vehicle and was immediately greeted by The Director himself, flanked by a pair of heavily armed bodyguards wearing black suits.

The Director greeted her, "Dina, good to see you unscathed."

This was one of the few instances Dina had encountered The Director in person, and his unexpected appearance caught her off guard. Any workers who were around and recognized him instantly doubled their working pace.

"Sir, it's a surprise to see you out here," Dina responded, doing her best to mask her anxiety.

"Judging by the recent attack, it appears we've stumbled upon something quite extraordinary," The Director noted, his gaze sweeping across the area.

"Where's Dr. Slotin?"

At the mention of the doctor's name, Dina's expression faltered. "He quit, sir. The pressure of the job got to him. He practically jumped out of the car the moment I left the base."

The Director's lips tightened in a thin line of disappointment. "That's unfortunate. Perhaps he'll reconsider. In the meantime, I'm eager to see his creation."

Just then, Thetor emerged from the truck, wounds visibly healing. His neck was wrapped in black, scale-like metal armor, and he towered over the surrounding men. The Director's eyes widened in awe as he approached.

"This must be him," The Director muttered, his tone echoing curiosity. Dina turned, recalling their earlier conversation about Jack. She watched Thetor anxiously, the memory still fresh in her mind. She knew she had to play her part convincingly.

"Yes, sir, this is him," she confirmed, gesturing towards Thetor. The Director reached out his hand, which Thetor met with a firm handshake.

"You must be The Director," he stated calmly. The Director stared up at him, amazed.

"We need to have a conversation. Dina, ensure the rest of the assets are appropriately distributed."

With a nervous nod, Dina watched as Thetor, The Director, and his bodyguards departed.

"Yes, sir," she responded, her voice softer than she'd intended. Once they were out of sight, Dina shook her head in disappointment, murmuring, "Shit," under her breath.

The crew worked diligently, moving the materials out of the trucks and into their designated rooms. Most of the parts had already been boxed up, but there were some larger pieces, such as a large section of the crashed craft's fin, that had to be moved as one piece. Finally, only one truck remained, the one carrying the bodies. Everyone had been avoiding it. Dina gestured to two men wearing full body coveralls. "You two, I want you to remove any advanced armor from the bodies. There should only be two sets. Then take the truck to the incinerator. They will know what to do."

Dina walked down the hallway that The Director and Thetor had walked down. She knew he would most likely have taken Thetor to the conference room. When she got to the room she looked through the glass window. Through the glass she could see them talking but wasn't able to hear the conversation. The Director

178

noticed Dina standing outside and walked toward the door then opened it.

"Dina I will have a meeting with you after, how about you have some food and a shower then we'll talk," he suggested.

Dina glanced down at her expensive suit and realized how dirty she had gotten. She was still wearing the large boots from the cleanup, and her pants were caked with a layer of thick dried mud. Her sport coat had tears from climbing through the jagged wreckage of the base and a layer of ash covered her entire outfit.

"Sounds good sir, thank you," she responded.

As Dina made her exit, she cast a backward glance, catching Thetor's intense gaze through the large glass windows of the meeting room. Once the door closed, and Dina was out of earshot, The Director returned to his seat at the large table with Thetor. His bodyguards stood motionless behind him.

"So, tell me more about this beacon," The Director initiated.

Meanwhile, within the confines of the ship, the interior lights cast a serene glow on Jack's bruised face. He stirred, a low groan escaping his lips as consciousness returned. The soft hum of the ship lured his eyes open. Blinking against the light, he reached for his phone to check the time: 10 A.M. Sunday. There was also a message from Sampson awaiting his attention, "We have a problem, call me when you can."

Taking a deep breath, Jack was relieved to find the pain in his ribs had subsided. He swung his legs off the bed and tiptoed out of the ship, careful not to rouse the others. Once he was inside the warehouse, he stretched, noting that he felt significantly better than he had before falling asleep.

"Nexo, I'm feeling great," he announced.

"I'm glad to hear I had been working all night to try and heal the more painful injuries."

Jack made his way to the table and chairs, sinking down onto one of them and propping his feet up on the table. He retrieved his phone and dialed Sampson, who answered after a few rings.

"Hey, what's the problem?" Jack asked.

Despite the sound of traffic in the background, Sampson's voice came through clearly on the line. "The problem is Thetor's location. They've moved everything to the base in upstate New York. I've only been there once, and it's a goddamn fortress."

Jack, seemingly unbothered, responded, "We have an alien spaceship. I doubt a base is going to be a problem."

Over the phone, Jack could hear Sampson pause, taking a deep breath. "Listen, Jack. The base is built into a mountain. It's where they store their best equipment, and they're heavily armed. The guns and armor they have make my gear seem like a water gun."

Something in Jack's demeanor shifted at Sampson's words. He removed his feet from the table, leaning forward. "Shit, what are we going to do then?"

"I'm on my way there now," Sampson informed him. "I'll gather some intel about the base and contact you later. And Jack? Don't do anything stupid."

Before Sampson could end the call, Jack interjected, "Wait! I have a question. The scientist at the base, Dr. Slotin was there, right?"

"Yeah," Sampson confirmed, "He was the head scientist. According to Dina, he quit. Why do you ask?"

Jack seemed excited at this. "Well, he's actually my boss. I think he likes me, so maybe he could help us."

Sampson's tone hardened at Jack's words. "Jack, Dr. Slotin is likely the most dangerous of them all. I'd stay clear of him. He's the one who experimented on my team. Just... wait for my call."

With that, Sampson hung up. Jack scratched his chin, musing aloud, "Nexo, what's your take on Dr. Slotin?"

"It's hard to say. Dr. Slotin had been kind to you in the past, yet if what Sampson is saying is true, he could have ulterior motives."

"I mean, I have known him for a long time, even before this promotion. He always just seemed really focused on his work, maybe he just got carried away?"

Dave suddenly stepped off the ship. "Who got carried away?" he asked.

Jack looked up at him as he came down the stairs. "Oh, you're awake. We were just talking about Dr. Slotin. He works with me at the factory, and when we were separated, I saw him at the base."

Dave walked over to the table and took a seat. "Is he cool?"

181

Jack simply shrugged. "I don't know him that well, but he seems nice. Although, I just spoke with Sampson, and he warned me not to trust him. He also mentioned we've got a problem."

Dave's eyebrows furrowed. "A problem?"

"Yeah, they moved everything to an insanely guarded base inside a mountain in upstate New York," Jack explained. "Sampson needs time to formulate a plan. He'll get in touch when he's ready."

Suddenly, Dave shot up, his frustration palpable. He paced back and forth, his brow knotted in deep thought. "So, what, we're supposed to just sit here and wait? We barely know this guy. Sure, he's our only lead, but he could be leading us into a trap. He might tell us to sit tight, only to show up with his squad in high-tech suits, ready to raid our hideout. Or they could just bomb us."

Jack reached out and gripped Dave's shoulders, trying to calm him. "Hey, chill, man. Just breathe. As you pointed out, if Sampson wanted us dead, he would've made his move by now."

His reality check working, Dave quickly composed himself. "Alright, but what about Dr. Slotin? You said you've worked with him. Maybe he knows something about the base. You're due at work tomorrow anyway. See what information you can get. He definitely didn't recognize you fully armored."

Jack shook his head, "Dave, knowing where the base is doesn't help without a plan. We should wait for Sampson."

Dave seemed to calm down more and suggested in a more relaxed tone, "How about this? We wait for Sampson's call, but in the meantime, see if you can find out anything from Slotin, just as a backup plan. What if something happens to Sampson or he gets discovered trying to help us? We need to be prepared for the worst."

Both men retook their seats, and Jack mulled over Dave's suggestion. "Alright, I'll head to work as usual. A backup plan could be useful," he agreed. Dave offered his hand and Jack responded with a lackluster high-five. Their shared laughter filled the room for a brief moment.

Just then, Z descended from the ship. "What's gotten you two so cheery?" he taunted. Jack retorted with a dose of sarcasm, "We're thrilled because I just got off the phone with Sampson, and we've realized how royally screwed we really are."

Z found a seat, his expression curious. "What do you mean 'screwed'?"

Dave chimed in, "Sampson says the base is pretty much impenetrable, so we can't use the ship. He's gonna figure out a plan and give us a call when he's ready."

Jack continued, "Also, Dave pointed out we should have a backup plan. Plus, I recognized someone at the base."

Z's head swung towards Jack when he heard this. "You knew someone at the base?"

Jack answered, "Yes, a Dr. Slotin. He managed to get out before you blew everything up. Sampson mentioned he quit after the attack, but also warned me not to trust him."

Dave interrupted, "Sampson just doesn't like him because he didn't get offered the serum. I bet he felt like it was because he's getting old."

Jack turned to Dave with his head tilted sideways. "He was young enough to kick your ass! Also, now that we were on the subject, I thought we were going to just take out Thetor, not blow up the whole base, you probably killed like six mercs."

Z had anticipated this discussion. "Look, you've seen my memories, you know what Omega can do. It's harsh, but sometimes people are just caught up in the wrong place at the wrong time."

Dave hung his head, speaking in a quiet tone. "Plus, we know for sure at least four of 'em had the nasty Synthrons. They'd have messed with their minds."

Jack rose, attempting to defuse the escalating tension. "Alright, let's just relax for a sec. If we stick to the plan, we're golden. I'll go to work tomorrow, try to chat up Dr. Slotin."

Dave yelled to Jack as he walked away, "You can't go to your apartment, remember they might still be watching it."

Jack yelled back as he headed out the door, "I know, I'm going to my parents' place."

CHAPTER 15 - THE LIE

Inside the mountain base, Dina had just finished her shower and was dressing in her private quarters when an unexpected knock echoed through the room.

"Give me a minute," Dina responded, only to be met with the sudden crash of the door being kicked in. Without warning, Dina found herself tackled to the ground.

"What the fuck are you doing?" she protested, as mercenaries swiftly bound her hands behind her back with zip ties. Once restrained, the room filled with the imposing presence of The Director and Thetor.

Seeing the two of them together, Dina immediately understood what had transpired. She made a desperate plea. "Sir, I've devoted years to this company. Don't listen to that thing; it's not even human."

Ignoring her, The Director knelt before her, a fat cigar clasped between his teeth. He took a puff then held the lit end close to her face. "Were you aware that your brother was the mastermind behind the attack?" he asked.

Dina's gaze fell to the floor. "I knew... but that knowledge wouldn't have changed anything."

Nonchalantly, The Director exhaled a puff of smoke towards her. Thetor remained a silent observer from the doorway.

"And where is your brother now? The second asset?" The Director demanded.

"I don't know, really," Dina replied, her voice trembling.

With a snap of The Director's fingers, the guards hauled Dina away. Her protests echoed through the corridor - "I don't know! I don't have any idea where he is!" Her desperate pleas gradually faded into silence as she was taken farther away.

Left alone in the room, Thetor turned towards The Director. "Sir, I may possess a method to extract the necessary information."

As he spoke, one of his fingers morphed into a long, slender syringe. The Director responded with a sinister smile.

Jack walked up the driveway to his parents' house and noticed his sister's car parked in the driveway. He also noticed his father's car was gone. Jack figured he was probably still at work. He knocked on the door and his mother answered, exclaiming, "Honey, what a surprise!"

Jack hugged his mother and walked inside. "Hi Mom, is Dina here?"

His mother looked confused for a moment before realizing the reason for Jack's question. "Oh, the car. No, some nice man from Dina's office dropped it off. He was actually asking about you, too, for some reason."

Jack tried to remain calm but peered out the blinds as his mother walked into the kitchen. "Asked about me, what did you tell him?"

Jack followed his mother to the kitchen as she replied, "Well, I told him I didn't know where you were."

Jack tried to play dumb as he sat down at the kitchen table. "Well that's weird. I'll have to ask Dina about that maybe."

His mother's face lit up. "Are you and your sister getting along again?"

Jack shrugged, "I don't know, she seems really busy with work."

Jack's mother grabbed a plate of cookies and slid them in front of Jack, "Here, I just made these."

Jack's mother then poured him a glass of milk and sat across from him. As he ate the cookies, she continued. "I know you and your sister dont always see eye to eye on everything, but I know she loves you. I want you to remember that."

Jack finished the rest of the cookie and washed it down with a sip of milk. "I know."

"So, what brings you here today?" Jack's mother inquired.

He had concocted an excuse during his walk over. "Oh, they're doing a bug spray in my apartment and the smell is just gross. Hope it's cool if I crash here for the night."

"Your room's always ready for you, Jack."

Jack spent some time catching up with his mom, and when his dad got home, they enjoyed a pleasant family dinner together. After their meal, Jack slipped away to his old bedroom. It was exactly as he had left it in his youth, making him feel oddly out of place, like a giant in a child's space.

"So this is your old room?"

"Yep, this is it," Jack replied as he looked through his old belongings.

He found a toy U.F.O. he used to play with. He picked it up and imagined it flying in the air. He chucked to himself. "Man, they didn't get this right at all."

Feeling tired, Jack decided to turn in early for the night. As he settled into his bed, he found himself mulling over Thetor's words during their recent fight.

"Nexo, what is your opinion on Thetor's theory about The Creators intentionally making Omega?" Jack asked.

"Based on the limited data I have on the beginning of the Synthron war, Thetor's explanation is not implausible. It is statistically more likely that Omega was designed rather than being a random glitch. However, we do not have enough information to determine The Creator's motives."

Jack looked out the window at the night sky while still lying down. "So, now you don't think Omega is a glitch?"

"It's strange, all my records from previous generations show Omega being faulty. Yet it is more probable that Omega was created by The Creators, but we do not know their purpose or intentions. Simply put, too much time has passed. However, we do know that Omega is imposing his goals on others without their consent."

Jack asked, "Do you believe anything Thetor said?"

"I don't have free will and, therefore, do not have the capacity for belief. I calculate probabilities based on available data. Currently, it is more likely that The Creators created Omega, but his original purpose is unknown. Additionally, it is more likely that Omega is killing people rather than downloading their consciousness."

Jack considered Nexo's response. "But isn't it possible that Omega is doing what he says?"

"From a philosophical perspective, nothing can be claimed with absolute 100% certainty. All knowledge relies on our perceptions and interpretations. From a scientific perspective, theories and hypotheses are also never considered 100% certain,

but rather supported by empirical evidence and subject to
revision based on new data."

Jack rolled over and closed his eyes. "I think I understand. Goodnight, Nexo."

"Goodnight, Jack."

The next morning, Jack woke up early and walked to the parking lot of his apartment complex. It was only about a half-hour away by foot, and he figured he had been gone so long that no one would be paying that close attention. He got into his car and drove to work. It had been a week since the last time he was at the factory, and to him, it felt like stepping into another world. Compared to the noise from the battle, the machines all seemed to run a bit quieter now. The volume on everything was turned down. The factory had not changed at all since the last time he was here yet Jack felt somehow it was different. He walked into the lab and was greeted by Dr. Slotin, "Jack, welcome back. I hope you had a good week off."

Jack had been out for a full week but so much had happened he had forgotten what excuse he gave. Jack just went along with it, casually nodding and replying, "Yes, it was good to have some time off."

Dr. Slotin proceeded to show Jack around the lab, explaining the various operations they conducted, mostly focused on developing new materials for a competitive edge. As Jack worked alongside Dr. Slotin throughout the day, he tried to think of a way to bring up the topic of the base without being too direct. Jack began to daydream, he imagined Dr. Slotin had a map with a dotted line leading to the base sitting on his desk. He was interrupted by Dr. Slotin, "Hey Jack, time for lunch. We usually eat on the side of the building, there is a nice shaded bench out there if you want to join us."

"Sure sounds good." Jack replied, then grabbed a snack from the vending machine before heading outside and sitting across from Dr. Slotin.

Jack started with some casual conversation, "It's really nice weather for lunch, isn't it?"

Outside was warm with a gentle breeze that carried the sweet scent of blooming flowers. The sun shone brightly in the sky. A few fluffy white clouds lazily drifted across the sky, and the tree above the group offered the perfect amount of shade. The gentle rustling of leaves and distant chirping of birds created a soothing background melody, perfect for a relaxing lunch break. Dr. Slotin looked around at the scenery then up at Jack, he nodded in agreement and added, "Reminds me of this one spot in upstate New York, I'd spend summers there."

Jack feigned nonchalance, "Oh yeah? Where's that?"

Dr. Slotin paused, lifting his gaze from his lunch, "I can't remember the town's name. Actually I worked there for a bit."

Jack, fighting off an unsettling feeling that Dr. Slotin could see right through him, decided to steer clear of the subject for the rest of the day, hoping to not arouse any suspicion. Post lunch, they all got back to their lab work. Despite his efforts to stay focused, Jack could not shake off the feeling of being watched by Dr. Slotin. He wrapped up the day's tasks and headed to his car, completely oblivious to Dr. Slotin subtly observing him from a distance. As Jack ignited the engine and pulled away, Dr. Slotin discreetly trailed behind, maintaining enough distance to avoid raising any alarms. Jack was too distracted by his thoughts to notice the car tailing him.

Jack parked outside of the warehouse and walked inside. Dr. Slotin parked down the road from a safe distance away and got out of the car quietly. He tiptoed through the tall overgrown grass that surrounded the warehouse making his way to the side where he spotted a broken window.

Inside the warehouse, Jack was greeted by Dave and Z. Dave looked up from his phone where he was watching skateboarding videos and asked, "How was work?"

"Not bad actually," Jack replied as he sat down at the table with the others.

"Any word from Sampson?" Z asked.

Jack shook his head and replied, "Unfortunately, no."

Dave closed his phone and stood up, frustration evident in his voice, "I'm sick of waiting around. While we're waiting for Sampson, they're probably building this thing already."

Unbeknownst to the group, Dr. Slotin had sneaked around to the side of the building. He peered through the window and was

192

able to see the ship, Dave, Jack and Z. He tucked his head back down and listened to the group's conversation.

Jack tried to calm Dave down, "We just have to wait. Sampson will call us and we'll go once we have a plan."

Outside the window Dr. Slotin heard Sampson's name. He remembered him from the temporary base. He pulled out his phone and texted, "I found them, also don't trust Sampson."

Pulling up the winding road to the mountain base, Sampson glanced at his phone, concerned by Dina's silence to his recent messages. He parked his black car next to the others, took in his surroundings, and saw The Director emerging from a glass door flanked by bodyguards. A sense of unease washed over Sampson as he went to meet him, uncertain of his intentions but sure it was not good news. The Director's stern expression deepened Sampson's dread.

"Mr. Sampson, we need to discuss a security breach," The Director announced, his grim countenance making Sampson's heart drop. He had a hunch about what was to follow.

"A security breach, sir?" Sampson asked, putting on an air of surprise. The Director, always calculating, always manipulating information to meet his ends, moved closer. "Yes, Dina has been compromised. It was her brother behind the attack."

Maintaining his act, Sampson echoed in disbelief, "She knew about the attack? And do we have any intel on the location of the second asset?"

The Director carefully scrutinized Sampson's response and seemed satisfied. "No, we don't know anything yet, but we are holding Dina for questioning. Thetor is with her now. Go drop off your things, and we will bring you up to speed."

Sampson hoisted a bag from the trunk of his car, its contents heavy with the weight of advanced armor and weaponry.

He felt a persistent unease as he ventured into a side hallway of the base. "Why would Thetor interrogate her?" he muttered to himself. He walked through a set of glass doors.

Navigating a lengthy corridor, he abruptly veered into a restroom. Once secluded in a stall, he sat on the toilet and locked the door. He took his phone from his pocket, his nimble fingers typed out a hasty message to Jack: "Your sister's been detained. They suspect her involvement in the attack. Thetor's conducting the questioning. The base is buzzing. We're located in Badger Creek, New York, tucked inside an old train tunnel. I'm devising a plan, but if I can't contact you, at least you'll know where to find us."

Sampson exited the stall and looked at himself in the mirror. He looked at the scars from past battles and smiled. He exited the bathroom then continued down the hallway to his room to drop off his bag. While walking he heard someone yell his name from behind, "Sampson!"

He turned to see Thetor in a full sprint towards him. Sampson realized he had been discovered. He dropped the bag he was carrying and pulled out the advanced gun inside. He fired at Thetor as he rushed toward him. Thetor was able to dodge the first two shots by darting left and right but the third hit him in the chest.

Thetor was sent flying back down the hallway, shattering the glass doors as he crashed through them. He landed in the main bay of the base only a few feet from The Director, who was being protected by a team of heavily armed bodyguards. The bodyguards quickly grabbed The Director and escorted him into a waiting black car, leaving Thetor behind.

Meanwhile, Sampson had run away from Thetor and hid in a small broom closet. He frantically opened the bag and tried to put on the Xenoscale armor. He could hear Thetor's heavy footsteps getting closer and closer, the sound of doors being kicked down becoming more frequent. Sampson knew that without the armor, Thetor would overpower him instantly. He quickly grabbed the chest-piece and pants, struggling to put them on in the cramped space. After a few tense moments of struggling, he finally managed to clamp the two halves of the suit together.

Sampson muttered in frustration, "They need to make this shit easier to get on in the next model."

But Sampson had no time to waste as he quickly clamped his boots in place, feeling the panic rising in his chest as he heard Thetor's footsteps growing louder. With a final grunt of effort, he activated his suit, feeling it hum to life as the systems came online. He reached into his bag for the last piece of his armor, the helmet, but accidentally knocked over a bucket in the small broom closet.

It crashed to the ground with a loud clatter causing him to freeze for a moment as he listened for any sound from outside. Sure enough, Thetor's footsteps were approaching, growing louder and louder. Panicking, Sampson quickly donned his helmet and secured it tightly in place. Just as he finished, Thetor burst through the wall of the closet with incredible force, tackling Sampson and hurtling them both through the wall and crashing into the laboratory beyond. The impact was so powerful that they crashed through several lab tables and equipment, causing the scientists inside the room to scramble for safety.

As one of the scientists left he hit the alarm on the wall next to the door. Alarms in the laboratory began to ring loudly and red emergency lights flashed throughout the room. Sampson stood up and looked at the large hole in the wall they had just crashed through, realizing that his weapon was still inside the closet leaning against the wall. Thetor had sprung onto a lab bench, his arms morphing into a pair of formidable blades. He lunged at Sampson, who deflected the strike with a piece of experimental metal conveniently located on a nearby lab bench. Seizing the moment, Sampson lunged at Thetor's ankles, yanking him off balance. Thetor toppled over, crashing into the array of glassware on the workbench beneath him. Sampson sprinted towards the closet and grabbed his gun as he ran through the hole in the wall. He turned around, and saw Thetor lunging forward towards him.

Sampson quickly shot at Thetor, missing his head by inches. Thetor tripped but recovered fast and charged again. Sampson was ready this time, rolling aside to dodge Thetor's bladed arm and landing in the hallway. He turned around and shot again, this time hitting Thetor's shoulder. The impact sent Thetor crashing through a wall into another room.

Dust clouded the air as Sampson followed him into the room, gun ready. But Thetor was waiting behind the door. He grabbed the gun's barrel and tossed it across the room. Now unarmed, Sampson traded punches with Thetor. After a few hits, Thetor landed a kick that sent Sampson sliding across the floor.

As Thetor approached, Sampson drew his sidearm and unloaded it on Thetor. Several of the bullets hit him in the chest and face but his armor was too thick for his normal pistol, each of the shots were deflected. Thetor remained standing, seemingly unfazed.

"You fight well, for a human," said Thetor as he towered over Sampon, who was lying on his back.

"Thanks, I've had some practice." Sampson replied as he spotted the more powerful gun on the other side of the room and quickly rolled over towards it. However, before he could reach it, Thetor lunged forward and struck him in the back with a long, thin blade, targeting a vulnerable part of his suit, the power supply. With the power source damaged and non-functional, Sampson felt the full weight of the suit as its systems shut down. Despite his compromised position, he managed to grab the gun and spin around, firing off a single shot. The blast grazed Thetor's face but it was not enough to stop him. Thetor swiftly disarmed Sampson, knocking the weapon out of his reach and discarding it. As the suit's systems completely shut down, Sampson found himself immobilized, trapped within its confines. With one swift movement, Thetor removed Sampson's helmet and callously cast it aside, leaving him vulnerable and defenseless. He turned his hand into a dagger-like blade and held it to Sampson's throat.

"I was going to keep you alive for questioning, but I have calculated that you are too dangerous," Thetor said.

Sampson smiled. "I'll take that as a compliment."

In a single, ruthless stroke, Thetor slit Sampson's throat, silencing him instantly. Sampson's hands shot up instinctively, desperately clutching at the gaping wound that spilled sanguine rivers. His eyes widened in horror as he struggled to breathe, the taste of his own blood suffocating him. Amidst the chaos, Thetor, resolute and focused, swiftly raised the front of his armor, positioning his blade for a final, decisive blow. With unwavering precision, he struck, piercing Sampson's heart, ending the turmoil and bringing an eerie calm to the scene. Thetor's expression remained stoic as he rose to his full height, he looked down on Sampson's lifeless form. The bright red glow of flashing lights bounced off the metallic components of his face. Thetor processed Sampson's death in less than a second, his demeanor unyielding and detached. A squad of armed mercenaries rushed into the room, only to find that Thetor had already neutralized the threat. The squad lowered their weapons as their squad leader radioed in, "The threat is eliminated. Disable the alarm."

As the blaring alarm subsided and the once-red lights faded away, returning the room to its usual fluorescent glow, Thetor pivoted to face the men.

"Clean this mess up," he ordered, then walked out of the room.

Thetor walked down the hallway to the last room and opened the door. Inside the room was Dina, who was strapped to a bed and confined in a clear bag. The bag contained Dr. Slotin's recipe, which he had used before to speed up the process. The black fluid was being pumped through the bag, and Dina's head was sticking out of the top. Dina looked at Thetor as he entered the room; she had heard the alarm and thought it might be Jack. She noticed Thetor's arms and body were covered in blood. Dina began to tear up. "What did you do?"

Her voice trembled as she asked. Thetor ignored her question and walked to the other side of the room to wash his hands in the sink. Dina watched him with rage in her eyes as he continued to ignore her.

"Didn't you hear me? I asked you what you did!" She yelled at him from her confined position.

Thetor dried his hands, then turned to her. "Silence," Thetor's voice resounded, void of emotion. "In due time, you shall unite with Omega, transcending pain and achieving eternal harmony."

Dina's eyes widened as she watched Thetor leave the room. She thrashed inside the bag and yelled, "Let me out of here!"

The door to the room slowly closed, and no one was left to listen.

CHaPTer 16 - THe New GUY

Inside the warehouse later in the evening Jack, Dave, and Z were all eating hamburgers. The group had decided they deserved a good meal so Dave had brought back some fast food from the next town over. Z looked down at the burger without taking a bite. It looked huge in his small blue hands, "Are you sure this is safe?" he asked.

"Z's species shouldn't have any problems digesting the contents of a hamburger."

Jack looked up at Z, "It should be fine. What have you been eating this whole time?"

Z inspected the burger more closely, taking off the bun then putting it back on, "Well I have had some extra food from my planet on the ship but I'm running low."

Dave had already finished his burger and moved on to the fries. He glanced over at Z's untouched burger and asked, "Are you going to eat that?"

Jack gave Dave a disapproving look. "Let him at least try it," he said to Dave before turning to Z. "Just take a bite, but don't take it all apart. It only works if you eat it together."

Dave looked at Z as he closed the burger. "Good. If I had to watch you disrespect a hamburger, I don't know what I would do."

Z looked up, confused. "Disrespect? You act like you worship these."

"Maybe some people do," Dave replied loudly, throwing his hands up in the air. Z pulled the hamburger up to his mouth and took a small bite.

He chewed slowly at first but then built up speed. After swallowing the first bite, he said, "Wow."

He resumed devouring the burger, talking with his mouth full. "Oh, wow, this is really good."

Jack and Dave looked on with mild disgust as Z's alien mouth scarfed down the food. Dave put his fries down on the table in front of him. Jack reached into his pocket and pulled out his phone to take a picture of Z. He snapped a photo of Dave and Z with their food. Z looked over at him, aiming his phone's camera at him, "What are you doing?" Asked Z, with a mouthful of food.

Jack quickly snapped a picture and said, "You'll want a picture of your first burger, trust me."

After taking the photo, Jack checked his phone and saw that he had received a text from Sampson a couple of hours ago. "Oh, Sampson texted me a couple of hours ago,"

Dave and Z both looked up with surprise. "A couple of hours ago! What does it say?" Dave exclaimed.

Jack read the message aloud, "Your sister's been detained. They suspect her involvement in the attack. Thetor's conducting the questioning. The base is buzzing. We're located in Badger Creek, New York, tucked inside an old train tunnel. I'm devising a plan, but if I can't contact you, at least you'll know where to find us."

Jack's eyes sank as he read the message, "Shit, they have Dina."

Dave looked across the table, "Well that's not good, I mean you did try to warn her."

"Jack if Thetor has Dina he will most likely try to inject her with a Synthron."

Jack got up from his chair and began pacing. "What should we do?"

Jack's voice filled with concern.

The group fell silent, each lost in thought, trying to come up with a plan. Z was the first to break the silence.

"Well, we know the location of the base. I'm sure there's only one abandoned tunnel in that town. That being said, I still think we should wait for Sampson to message us."

Jack's expression turned even more worried. "I don't know. If Dina is captured, Thetor will probably inject her with a Synthron."

Z's face took on a somber look as he replied, "If he was going to inject her, he probably already has."

Jack pounded his fist on the table. "Well, we have to do something!"

Outside the warehouse, Dr. Slotin remained by the window, still listening intently. He slowly backed away and walked to his car, driving off into the night. Dr. Slotin pulled out his phone and made a call, "Hey, I have a plan for how to fix our problems."

Inside the warehouse, the group continued to discuss options for some time until Jack received a text from Sampson. Jack looked down at his phone. "Wait, I just got another text from Sampson."

Dave and Z moved closer to Jack, Dave said, "Read it aloud."

So Jack did. "I have a plan. Have Dave drive to the front gate. I signed him up as a new hire. You can find the gate at the back of Longview Drive in Badger Creek."

Dave stepped back from the group, "That's his plan? To have me walk right in there?"

Jack squinted as he stared at his phone screen. "That does sound odd. Perhaps I should give him a call," he suggested.

Jack picked up the phone and dialed Sampson's number, but after only one ring, he was greeted with a pre-recorded message: "We're sorry, but the person you're trying to reach has not set up their voicemail box. Please try again later."

"Damn it!" Jack exclaimed in frustration. "Straight to voicemail."

Z and Jack both looked at Dave, waiting for a decision. Dave spoke up, "I'll do it. Maybe he can't answer the phone or has no service down there. He may need someone to help him get Dina out of there before we blow the base up or something."

Z and Jack each gave Dave a reassuring pat on the back. "That's the spirit," Jack commended, adding with a light-hearted grin, "Hell, you're the one who got me into this mess!"

Dave laughed, "Oh, like you didn't need any help. Fine, if I leave now I can get there by morning. I'll take my car. Jack, I want that ringer of yours on the loudest setting."

Jack gave Dave a thumbs up, "We will park the ship nearby and come in at the first sign of trouble. I want you to text me right when you go in, then text me updates so I know you're okay."

Dave grabbed his things and headed towards the door. Jack gave him a hug and said, "Be safe. The first sign of trouble, you bail."

He got into his car and drove away. Jack and Z walked back to the ship. Z said, "Let's get an early sleep. We will leave early in the morning."

Jack and Z climbed into the ship and laid down. Both of them had their eyes wide open but tried not to think about tomorrow. Jack rolled to his side and looked at Dave's empty bed.

"Jack, I wanted to let you know if they did inject Dina with a Synthron, there may be a way to save her. I'll tell you tomorrow. Get some sleep."

Nexo then helped Jack fall asleep quicker, so he could get a full night's rest.

The next morning Jack was jolted awake by a slight bump. Z was at the front of the ship flying. Jack swung his legs off the bed and stood up and walked to the front of the ship holding onto the sides of the ship as he walked. When Jack got to the front of the ship he sat in the seat he normally sits in off to the side.

Z turned his head and noticed Jack was awake, "Hey, I figured I'd let you sleep there."

"Thanks." Jack replied in a still half asleep tone yawning. He looked out the window and was met with the sunset just peeking over the trees in front of them.

"Hey don't we need to go west?"Jack asked.

Z turned his head back, "Well I actually already found it. I just needed to find a spot to land where they wouldn't find us. There is a field about a half mile away that looks promising. I was able to stay low so they shouldn't even know we're here."

The Luxastra made a final sharp turn and landed next to some trees in a flat open field. It was at the top of a hill that had a good view of the entrance to the base. Once on the ground, the silver exterior began to shake violently, and a loud grinding noise filled the grassy field as the morning sun kissed the mirror-like surface of the ship. The metal twisted and folded, but this time it took the appearance of a large boulder. The side of the rock opened, and Jack and Z stepped out. The pair set up a small camp next to the rock. Z opened a backpack and started putting on clothing with the tags still attached. Jack looked at Z while unfolding a chair and chuckled, "What are you doing?"

Z looked up at Jack, "Dave got me these," he exclaimed, holding up the clothes, "He said they would help me blend in."

Jack looked down at Z as he put on an oversized baseball cap, to hide his ruffled head. Jack read what was on his shirt aloud, "Skateboarding rocks?"

Z looked upset by Jack's judgment, "Listen, it was better than nothing."

Jack reached forward and ripped the tag that was hanging off the shirt while he shook his head, "Dave better call us before anyone finds us, or we're screwed."

About a mile away Dave was inside his car at a gas station. He looked in the mirror and checked his hair. He picked his phone up that was resting in the cup holder: "About to head in now, I'll call you when I can."

Jack texted back immediately: "Sounds good, we'll be ready."

Dave started his car and pulled out onto the road. He followed the GPS turning down a smaller road then turned once more onto what looked like a service road only wide enough for one vehicle to fit at a time. Dave was driving uphill and approached a gate with two armed guards. The guard to the left held out his hand.

"Stop right there." Dave rolled down his window and the guard approached,

"What business do you have here?" The guard asked with a stern tone. The second guard circled the car with a mirror on a long stick checking the underside of the vehicle for any explosives. Dave responded politely, "I'm a new hire, I'm supposed to report to Sampson."

The two guards looked at one another then they both backed away from the car. The guard with the mirror opened the gate while the other said, "Okay drive straight into the main bay at the top of the hill, he will meet you there."

Dave pulled through the gate and glanced in the mirror, he was able to see one of the guards on the radio. He quickly turned the rear view mirror at himself. He could see sweat beads accumulated on his forehead. He promptly wiped them off. He looked at his nervous face once more, "You just work here Dave, you can do this. You belong here."

He told himself as he continued driving up the steep slope. Once at the crest of the hill he could see the entrance, a large hole cut out of the side of the mountain with several armored vehicles and men standing in front. He continued to drive towards the opening. One of the armed men waved him through. As Dave's car slowly crept forward the man yelled as he passed, "Drive straight down the tunnel, someone will direct you once you reach your destination."

Dave gave a thumbs up and waved as he past by the group. He continued down the long tunnel passing many parked cars and people walking. Dave drove slow and looked closely at each person so he wouldn't miss Sampson waving for him. Soon Dave had passed most of the people and was entering a part of the tunnel that seemed more vacant. Less people were around and Dave began to fear he had gone too far. Dave stopped the car and opened the door. He turned off his car and stepped out. He then looked around, but no one was there. Dave scratched his head. "Maybe I passed him?"

Suddenly a loud noise filled the tunnel, the sound echoed off the concrete walls. A massive metal door was closing behind him sealing him in. Dave struggled to maintain his composure as the door closed behind him, locking with a resonant clang. Once the door was closed the light from outside was no longer able to be seen and only small yellow lights illuminated the space. The large doors also sealed off the space from sound causing Dave to feel uncomfortable with the silence. Dave yelled out, "Hello!"

Only to hear his echo yell back from the tunnel, "Hello. Hello. Hello."

Then Dave thought he heard something, he listened closely. Someone was in the distance approaching from deep within the tunnel. Dave could tell they were getting closer. "Sampson? Is that you?"

Dave could see a figure but it was too dark. He reached in his car and hit the lights to illuminate them. Dave looked up and the first thing he noticed was a distinctive metallic jaw. Dave feared the worst but held on to the hope that this was a coincidence. He did not want to give himself up quite yet. Dave put on a nervous smile as Thetor continued walking towards him. "Hey, I must be lost. I just got hired. I'm looking for Sampson. Do you know where he is?"

Thetor stopped walking and cracked his neck, "You're not lost Dave, you're exactly where you're supposed to be."

As Thetor spoke his arms slowly transformed into two long blades. Dave instantly broke out in a cold sweat; he knew this was all a setup. He fumbled for his phone in hopes of sending a message to the others but he was too deep within the tunnel to get any service. Thetor watched him as he struggled, "No bars?"

Thetor propelled himself forward with a burst of speed towards Dave. On his approach, Dave responded by triggering the motor units coursing through his system to armor his body with the black metallic scales. Instead of confronting Thetor head on, he swiftly sidestepped, allowing the charging Thetor to barrel past him.

Undeterred, Thetor whirled around for a second attempt, with a predatory snarl, he launched himself towards Dave once again.

However, this time, Dave did not evade. Instead, he transformed his arms into gleaming black blades of Synthron steel.

Thetor responded with an arm morphed into a large axe, slashing down towards Dave. With a swift movement, Dave parried the attack to one side with his own blade-arm, the resulting clash sent sparks flying in the dim light. He swiftly threw a slash of his own, aiming for Thetor's midsection. Thetor skillfully sidestepped, retaliating with a series of rapid powerful axe swings that Dave managed to block and deflect with his own weapons.

Despite his dexterity, Dave could feel the disadvantage of his situation. Thetor was relentless, his strength seemingly inexhaustible, while Dave could feel his own energy beginning to drain.

Recognizing his need for a strategic retreat, Dave lashed out one last time, a sharp, quick slash aimed at Thetor's face. Thetor recoiled, the attack leaving a shallow cut across his cheek. Seizing this momentary distraction, Dave disengaged from the melee. He launched himself towards the imposing door.

Dave transformed his arm into a crowbar. Every muscle in his body strained as he leveraged against the uncooperative barrier. His concentration was so focused on the door that he failed to sense the imminent danger behind him.

Before Dave could react, Thetor's powerful grip squeezed him from behind. The world spun as he was hoisted off his feet and then violently introduced to the cold, hard floor beneath him. The impact reverberated through his skull with a loud crack, leaving him momentarily winded and stunned.

Dave scrambled to his feet, breathing heavily. His ears rang from the devastating blow to his head. He saw Thetor coming closer and quickly bolted into the depths of the tunnel. This wasn't just a tunnel, but a maze filled with large crates of food, uniforms, and other supplies. He ran hard, weaving around stacks of crates, his heart pounding in his chest.

But Thetor was close behind. Dave could hear his footsteps growing louder. He glanced over his shoulder to see him getting closer. Panic surged through him. He was running out of room - the tunnel was becoming narrower, the stacks of supplies growing taller.

Finally, he was trapped. Backed into a tight metal hallway, he watched as Thetor approached, his arm-blades scraping against the walls, throwing sparks into the air.

"Nowhere to run now, Dave," Thetor said. Dave's heart pounded in his still ringing ears.

"My friends will come for me," he managed to say. Thetor just smiled.

"I hope they do," he replied, before pressing a button on the wall.

Suddenly, Dave was surrounded by a blinding light and an electric jolt coursed through him. When his vision returned, he was trapped within a clear, glowing force field. He pounded on the field, but it was impenetrable.

A new voice came from behind Thetor. "Good work."

Dr. Slotin appeared from the shadows, several armed men behind him. Thetor turned to face him.

"Your device worked great. I'm impressed."

Dr. Slotin looked at Dave in his cage. "We found this technology in a crashed ship in South America. Seems like it was used for carrying prisoners."

Thetor nodded. "Take him to the other prisoner," he ordered, his eyes fixed on Dave.

The men took Dave to the room Dina was in and placed his cage on the far side. Dina watched, her body trapped inside her clear bag as they left, and the two were left alone. Dave stood up and looked around, and then turned to face Dina. Dave looked over as the black fluid pumped through tubes and into the bag Dina was trapped inside only her head poked out the top.

"Hey, what are they doing to you?" Dave asked.

"They're trying to get information out of me," Dina replied, as her body writhed inside the confined space.

Struggling to concentrate, Dave recognized the voice from a phone call he'd overheard between her and Jack. "Wait a minute... aren't you Jack's sister?" he questioned, disbelief evident in his tone.

Dina replied with a hint of annoyance, "Yes, that's me."

A laugh began to bubble up from Dave. "Your brother has been trying to tell you how messed up these guys are for ages," he said, shaking his head.

Dina grew more irritated and rolled her eyes. "You know what? Screw you," she snapped. "This is probably the first time my brother has been right about anything in a long time. You don't know him like I do. Jack has done terrible things in the past when he was an addict, so I'm sorry if I don't believe everything he says."

Dave's laughter subsided. "Jack has done terrible things. Like what?"

Dina shook her head. "I have a long list, but I'll give you an example. A few months ago, my mom couldn't find her wedding ring. She thought she had lost it and blamed herself. I knew it was Jack, so I confronted him about it. He wouldn't admit it to me, but I could tell he was lying. So I went to a pawn shop in the next town over and found her ring there. I bought it back for her and just told her that I found it. The thing is, I wanted to tell my mom what happened, but I knew that Jack stealing from her would break her heart way more than losing the ring, so I just let it go."

Dave looked at Dina with disappointment in his eyes. "I'm sorry, I didn't know it had gotten that bad. Listen, I know Jack might have messed up things in the past, but that's all behind him now. He's trying to make things right."

A small tear rolled down Dina's cheek as she thought about how she had ignored Jack. But her sadness quickly changed into anger. "So what's the plan now? I'm guessing it wasn't to get captured."

Dave pounded his fist on the force field. "Yeah, you got that right. I was supposed to meet a guy named Sampson here, but then I was ambushed."

Dina thought back to when Thetor was covered in blood. "I think they must have discovered Sampson's plan to help you. I heard what sounded like fighting, then Thetor came in here and was covered in blood."

Dave looked confused, "Well if it wasn't Sampson or you that double crossed us then who?"

Inside of the meeting room within the base the door swung open. Thetor along with Dr. Slotin walked inside and sat down at the table with The Director. His bodyguards stood at the back of the room but did not make eye contact with anyone. Thetor spoke as he walked in the room, "The first threat has been neutralized. We believe there to be one more along with the enemy ship and its pilot."

The Director looked pleased, "Well done Dr. Slotin on getting the cage operational for our friend here, can I ask what brought you back?"

Dr. Slotin turned to The Director."I realize I may have acted too harshly, and Thetor has a way of convincing people."

The Director nodded. "Well, it's good to have you back. Thetor, go check on the new prisoner and see if you can get him to bring the others here, hopefully with the asset intact."

Thetor's emotionless face turned to The Director. "Will do. I should kill the prisoner after we use him."

The Director quickly said, "No, I don't want him killed. We need to study him more."

Thetor got up and left the office, leaving The Director and Dr. Slotin alone. Once the door closed and Thetor walked down the hall, The Director spoke up. "So tell me the truth. Should we trust this beacon that he wants us to build?"

Dr. Slotin used a television screen on the wall to pull up the blueprints. "These are the blueprints that Thetor has presented to us," he said as he flipped through the screens, "I have gone over them, and as far as I can tell, this device will do what he said. It should provide more energy than any other known means. This could be a huge boost for humanity as a whole."

The Director picked up a cigar sitting next to him and cut off the tip using a gold-plated cigar cutter. "Why is it that these other people are so intent on keeping this device from being built?"

Dr. Slotin turned his head away from the screen and looked back at The Director. "The way Thetor has explained it to me is that this species doesn't want this form of energy production to proliferate. It's similar to the way nuclear energy is kept from countries due to the fear of nuclear weapons. The humans that are

215

aiding this species must have been deceived in some way, or perhaps they are being paid."

The Director lit his cigar and took a couple of puffs. He then stood up and walked to the television screen, inspecting the prints closely. The prints showed a device that looked like a sphere but had many layers and intricate components. The Director inspected the prints closely but did not have the engineering background to understand what he was looking at.

"I just want to be on the right side of history," he said, turning back to Dr. Slotin.

"Make sure you and your team comb through these blueprints before anything is turned on. I'm going to head back to New York."

He paused before adding, "Also, until I find a replacement for Dina, you're in charge of the Acquisitions department. Make sure Thetor stays in line."

Dr. Slotin nodded in agreement. "Understood, we'll be sure to thoroughly examine the blueprints and ensure that everything is in order before activating the device."

The Director picked up his briefcase with his cigar still in his mouth and headed towards the door. "Good luck. And remember, we need to handle this with care."

With that, The Director left the room along with his bodyguards.

CHAPTER 17 - THE MOUNTAIN

Jack and Z watched the base's entrance from a vantage point, about a half-mile away on a hill. Through the trees, they could see the base with an opening halfway up the adjacent hillside, located across a narrow valley. A road sliced through the center of the valley, stretching between them and the base. They used their enhanced eyesight to inspect the defenses in front of the large opening in the mountain.

Two trucks were parked in front of the entrance with several armed guards. Looking closely, they could see more guards inside the tunnel, but the bulk of them appeared to be guarding the entrance. Z turned to Jack and asked, "So, how do you think they're doing?"

Jack refocused his eyes from the great distance and replied, "I don't know, but I'm beginning to worry. He should have messaged us by now."

"Jack, we need to establish a backup plan if Dave or Sampson don't contact us."

Jack stood up and said, "Let's get back to the ship. If we get spotted, we're screwed."

Z followed him as they walked up the slight slope through the tall grass. Jack asked, "So what time do we move on to plan B?"

Z, who was so short that the grass was taller than him, turned one arm into a blade and sliced through the thicker sections as the midday sun beat down on them.

"I think if we don't hear anything by nightfall, we'll have to move in. If we can get you a uniform and I go inside a backpack, we might be able to get past the guards."

"I noticed the guard at the front gate at the bottom of the hill is usually by himself, sometimes there are two at most," Jack replied.

Z nodded his head and smiled. "That could work."

Both of them quickly made their way to the ship, which was still disguised as a large rock. Jack looked around the area to ensure that no one was around, and then he opened the door, allowing them both to climb inside. The side of the ship closed behind them, concealing the entrance.

Back inside the base, Dave and Dina were in one of the laboratories. Dina was still strapped to the bed, and Dave was locked within the forcefield cage. They were talking when the door suddenly swung open, slamming the wall and interrupting their conversation. Thetor walked through the door and strode quickly towards Dave.

"So it's time we invite your friends," Thetor said, pacing in front of the cage. Although incapable of feeling anger, Thetor understood the appearance of being angry when using intimidation tactics. Dave sat inside the cage with his legs crossed and looked up at Thetor as he walked in front of the cage.

"I don't think they will want to come to your party," Dave said mockingly. However, his tone turned serious as he stood up to face Thetor. "Also, if I don't call soon, they are going to know something is off."

Thetor stopped walking and looked down at Dave with disgust. "If you want any hope of getting out of this alive, I suggest you play along. I'm going to call Jack, and you're going to tell him that he can come to the front gate. These games you're playing need to end. You don't even understand the technology that you're using."

Dave looked down, shaking his head. "So, you'll let me go if I convince Jack to come to the front gate?"

From across the room, Dina began to yell. "Dave, don't listen to him!"

In response, Thetor extended a long, thin blade from his arm, slicing Dina's cheek. "Quiet, or I'll slit your throat next."

Blood began to drip from the fresh cut. Dina closed her eyes and turned her head away.

Turning back to Dave, Thetor calmly responded, "To answer your question, yes, I'll let you go. I merely wish to converse with your friends and gain access to the asset. This entire conflict has been one massive misunderstanding."

Dave gave a nod of understanding. "Fine, I'll call him." He pulled his phone from his pocket and turned on the screen, only to find no service. With a hint of sarcasm in his voice, he snipped, "No bars, big guy."

Thetor leaned over to the control panel on the cage and pressed several buttons. "Your phone's signal shouldn't be blocked any longer."

Dave dialed Jack, who picked up on the first ring. "Dave, what's up? How's it going in there?" Jack inquired.

Frantic, Dave attempted to warn Jack. "Jack, it's a trap! Sampson is dead, and both Dina and I are captive. Thetor's running the whole base!" he shouted into the phone.

Thetor quickly hit a button on the control panel that blocked Dave's phone signal, ending the call. Thetor paused for a moment then slowly stood up straight, his face emotionless. "You're going to regret that decision Dave," he said coldly.

Thetor abruptly turned and walked out of the room. Dave looked at his phone and slid it back into his pocket then turned to Dina and inspected the large laceration on her cheek. "You okay?"

"Yeah, I'm fine," as Dina answered, the large slash on her face began to close at a rapid rate. Dave watched as the wound sealed before his eyes.

"What's with the black fluid you're in? What does it do?" Dave asked, his gaze focused on the tubes pumping the dark substance.

Dina replied, "It accelerates the integration process. Our lead scientist, Dr. Slotin, used it before. It took what would've been two weeks down to three days."

"And how long have you been in there?"

Dina shrugged, "I've lost track. There are no windows or clocks in here. I'm guessing a day, maybe two."

Dave's expression faltered. "You know the Synthron he injected isn't like ours."

Dina shook her head, her tone somber, "I know."

Dave tried to uplift the mood, "Hey, I just warned Jack. I bet he's gonna burst through the door any moment now."

Dina averted her gaze. She understood that it was only a matter of time before her thoughts weren't her own anymore. As she contemplated the implications, she found herself wondering if she'd even survive the Synthron's integration process. Dave noticed her distress and attempted to distract her.

"So, given that you're technically unemployed now, have you thought about what you'll do when this is over?"

Dina laughed, turning her head back towards Dave, "Guess you're right. I do need to find a new job. I haven't given it much thought. What about you?"

Dave crossed his legs and sat down in the cage, "Well, once all this is over, I'm heading to Florida. Perfect skateboarding weather all year round."

Dina smiled faintly, "Florida sounds nice. I've had to be so straight-laced for so long. This job was everything to me. I made so many sacrifices to climb the ladder. Look where it got me. Maybe it's time I tried relaxing for a change."

Outside Jack and Z were frantic after receiving the call. Jack was pacing the ship, "Shit, shit, shit."

Z's head was down as he tried to think.

"Jack, If we can get inside and free Dave we will have an extra number."

Jack spoke to Z, "If we free Dave it will be three against one."

Z cast a glance at Jack, replying in a somber tone, "I have an idea." He rose and made his way towards the rear of the ship.

"What?" Asked Jack. Z opened a compartment in the rear of the ship and two sets of vials were inside the compartment. Z pulled out two small tubes. One was glowing a brilliant blue and the other was devoid of any color, the inside looked blacker than anything Jack had ever seen. Jack watched as he pulled out the tubes carefully and placed them inside a fanny pack. The two containers clanked into one another as he placed them inside and Z flinched.

"Sorry this is what powers the ship," Z explained as he carefully secured the two vials then closed the compartment that the remainder of the vials were in.

"That's the ship's store of element 115 and its antimatter counterpart, it is what powers the ship's FTL capabilities, an unregulated combination would cause quite a large explosion."

"Nexo, how large?" Jack asked under his breath as Z clipped the fanny pack around his back.

"Only one gram of antimatter with one gram of matter is equivalent to the energy released by the detonation of 43 kilotons of TNT, which is roughly equivalent to the energy released by an atomic bomb."

"Z, are you sure about this? Looks like more than a gram," Jack expressed, his concern evident, as they stood at the rear of the ship. Unfazed, Z moved past Jack, heading to the ship's front and then towards the exit.

"Once the containers are combined, the fuel decays rapidly. We're lucky if even a tenth reacts," Z said, stepping off the ship with Jack trailing behind him. "Let's get to work."

They positioned themselves at a vantage point, laying out a strategy to infiltrate the base. Z indicated towards a hill base with a stationed guard.

"That's our entry point. We'll wait for the shift change, nab the incoming guard's uniform. That gives us maximum time before detection," Z outlined.

Using his augmented vision, Jack studied the guard meticulously. "Alright, sounds good," he agreed.

For hours, they lay in wait, watching the sun make its journey across the sky and disappear behind the trees. Z kept a vigilant eye on the guard, observing his descent down the hill towards the front gate guards. Nudging Jack, Z pointed it out. "Time to move, the shift's changing."

Under the shelter of darkness, they made their way down the hill. Sprinting down the steep slope, they sought refuge behind a guardrail on the opposite side of the service road leading to the gate. As a car's headlights pierced the darkness, they crouched lower. Once the vehicle zoomed by, they leaped over the guardrail, sprinted across the road, and merged into the forest.

Nestled in nearby bushes, they watched as the descending guard approached his counterpart at the gate.

"About time, you're fifteen minutes late," the gate guard grumbled.

"Sorry, had some ice cream earlier. Messed with my stomach," the relief guard apologized.

The gate guard, grabbing his bag, retorted as they swapped places, "I don't get why you eat dairy; you know it's lethal every time you eat it. You better be fifteen minutes early tomorrow."

With that, he started up the hill, his backpack swaying with each step.

Z turned to Jack, "Let's tail him."

Jack and Z followed the guard up the hill, sticking to the trees and moving quickly but quietly. When the guard turned around, he heard someone approaching from behind and said, "Jesus Bill, do you need to use the shitter again?"

Jack quickly closed in and surprised the guard with a punch, knocking him unconscious. As the guard fell to the ground, Jack could not resist making a quip.

"Not exactly," he said in a comical tone, satisfied with the successful takedown. Z rolled his eyes but could not help but smile at Jack's humor. They swiftly donned the guard's uniform, stowed the bound guard in a cluster of nearby bushes, and then proceeded towards the base, prepared to resume their covert mission. Soon they were within eyeshot of the front door. Z climbed inside the backpack that they stole from the guard and Jack threw it on his back.

"Ouch be careful!" Z said as the bag smacked against his back. Jack looked back at the bag, "Oh, sorry."

Jack got on the dirt path and walked up the hill trying to act natural. He pulled his hat down to try and hide his face as much as possible.

"Remember Jack the larger the corporation, the easier to infiltrate. Just stay calm and if they ask you questions, say you're new and play dumb."

225

"Okay here we go." Jack said under his breath as he continued to march up the hill towards a large collection of armed guards and mercenaries. As Jack walked past one of the large trucks one of the guards yelled down to him, "What took you so long?"

Jack quickly answered back, "That idiot Bill ate dairy again. He was late to his shift."

The guard laughed, "Fuckin Bill."

Jack kept walking at a steady pace, moving past the collection of guards without stopping. He soon found himself within the base and paused to take in the impressive structure. Scientists and workers bustled about, moving materials in all directions.

"Jack, keep moving. You don't want to stand out."

Jack continued down the long tunnel, with large doors branching out on each side.

"Nexo, it could be any one of these. There are so many."

"Well, just try one, and we'll go through systematically."

Jack turned right and walked into the largest door he saw. Inside, workers were constructing a large spherical structure. Jack continued forward, dodging sparks from welders as they framed together the structure. He took a closer look at what they were building.

"Jack, they're making a beacon."

"That's a beacon?" Jack asked, surprised.

"Yes, it looks like Thetor has convinced them to construct it. Once complete, it will send a quantum signal to Omega, and he will become aware of Earth's existence."

226

"Shit," Jack muttered under his breath. He continued forward, stepping over construction materials. Suddenly, he kicked a large metal beam resting on the ground, causing it to clank loudly against the other beams. Several workers in hard hats quickly turned and looked at him. One of them yelled out, "Hey you lost?"

Jack turned and walked away, "Oh sorry, wrong room." Jack walked back into the large tunnel.

"Maybe try asking someone."

Jack approached one of the workers operating a forklift, he had to yell so the operator could hear him.

"Hey, Thetor wants me to drop this off with the prisoners. Do you know where they are?"

The operator turned the forklift engine off, "That guy gives me the fucking creeps, I keep seeing him walk in and out of the room in the back left corner of the tunnel, they might be in there."

The operator then nodded towards the bag. "What are you bringing him anyway?"

Jack started walking away, "I didn't ask."

The operator turned the engine back on and continued working as Jack quickly walked away, "I didn't ask. What a tool." The operator said under his breath.

One of the engineers inside the room with the beacon walked out of the large doors and approached the forklift operator, asking, "Hey, what did that guy ask you?"

The operator turned off the motor once again and replied, "He wanted to know where the prisoners were."

Suddenly, the engineer's expression changed and he quickly ran over to a red button on the wall, pushing it. He picked up a phone next to the button and spoke urgently into it, his voice echoing throughout the complex over loudspeakers, "Intruder alert! There is an intruder in the base. He is dressed as a mercenary and carrying a backpack."

Alarms blared throughout the entire compound, sending scientists and workers scrambling out of the base. The mercenaries guarding the front of the base ran inside and began searching for the intruder. One mercenary, who was also carrying a backpack, was searched and questioned by the others who didn't recognize him. Jack heard the alarms and knew he had to move fast. He began running through the base, dodging workers and equipment as he went.

Dina and Dave also heard the alarms blaring throughout the compound, still confined within the laboratory. Dina turned to Dave with worry etched on her face, "It must be Jack!"

Suddenly, the door to the laboratory burst open and Thetor walked in. He quickly approached Dave's cage and hit a button on the control panel, causing it to send a violent shock through the cage. Dave screamed in pain as he convulsed and collapsed to the ground. Dina was horrified as she saw Dave's motionless body, "Dave!"

Thetor turned and looked at Dina with a smirk on his face as he left the room, "I told him he would regret that."

CHAPTER 18- THE HALLWAY

Jack made his way out of the main tunnel and into a door that led to a labyrinth of hallways. He continued running down the hallway towards the back left corner of the base, Z was getting tossed around inside the backpack. He tightly hugged the fanny pack, trying to keep his balance.

"Hey, be careful out there!" Z shouted to Jack. Jack tightened the backpack straps and tried to run more smoothly.

"Just be ready to help," Jack replied, maintaining a brisk jog. He passed one room with smashed walls and wondered what happened but continued moving. As he approached the end of the hall, Jack began opening doors to check for Dina and Dave. The first room was empty, and the next had two scientists hiding behind a corner. When Jack flung the door open, one of them screamed in fear. Trying to maintain his cover, Jack spoke in a gruff voice, "Sorry ma'am, just clearing rooms. You need to evacuate immediately."

The two scientists quickly grabbed some items from their desk and scurried past Jack. He exited the room and continued down the hallway, checking several more rooms. He continued searching until he reached the last door at the end of the hall, which was much larger than the others. As he neared the massive door, Jack heard a strange sound above him. He stopped and glanced up, but saw nothing. Suddenly, the ceiling collapsed on him, sending shards of tiles flying everywhere. Jack had no time to react before Thetor crashed down on him, breaking through the tiles. Jack fell to the floor and the backpack containing Z flew out of his grasp. Thetor towered over him, grinning wickedly.

"Nice to see you, Jack!" he boomed, before morphing his arm into a huge hammer. He swung it at Jack's stomach, sending him skidding across the ground. Jack got up quickly and faced Thetor. The large door was right behind him, and Jack knew he had made it to the right place. He locked eyes with Thetor, who stood in the way.

"I have a surprise for you this time," Jack said.

Thetor's eyes narrowed. "A surprise?"

Without warning, Z burst out of the bag and clung onto Thetor's face. His little fists punched with incredible force as Z used all his might. Jack spotted a chance and sprinted towards the two. He aimed for Thetor's knees and tackled them with his full weight, pushing them through the large door that led to the room. Dina's scream pierced the air as they barged in. Thetor, Jack, and Z skidded on the floor and landed in a heap. Jack quickly scanned the room and saw the horrifying sight, Dina was trapped in a clear bag with her head sticking out the top and Dave laid motionless in a force field cage that zapped him every few seconds.

Jack did not waste any time and sprang to his feet. He darted towards Dina and sliced open the thick clear plastic. The thick black liquid oozed out onto the floor as her slimy body started to wriggle out. Z and Thetor were still fighting as Dina tried to get free. Jack glanced over at Z and he seemed to be doing well against Thetor so he dove towards the cage next.

"The control panel on the bottom. The red button should free him."

Jack spotted the red button and pushed it. The force field flickered and vanished, freeing Dave from the electric shocks. Dina finally wriggled out of the bag and tried to walk towards them, but she kept slipping on the black liquid that had filled the bag and soaked the floor around her. Jack pulled Dave's limp body out of the cage and laid him on the floor. He checked his pulse and saw he was still alive, but barely. He turned to Dina and shouted, "Get him out of here! Now!"

Jack looked back at Z and Thetor who were locked in a fierce battle. They were flying across the room, throwing punches and kicks at each other, every hit landed with a loud thud. They almost hit Dina as she stumbled towards the door, dragging Dave with her. Jack jumped towards them and grabbed Thetor by the throat. All three of them crashed into the back wall of the laboratory, which was made of solid concrete. The impact was so strong that it cracked the wall. Concrete dust and black flakes from their armor flew everywhere. Dina continued to drag Dave out of the room and into the hallway. She dragged him down the hallway but she soon heard footsteps approaching. The footsteps were from eight mercenaries, two of them were leading the charge wearing Xenoscale armor. One of them saw Dina and pointed at her, "Grab her."

Several mercenaries gabbed at Dina; she fell backwards as they grabbed her and she kicked one of them in the face, breaking his nose. Four of the men stayed with Dina while the other four rushed ahead towards the large smashed door. The mercenary with a broken nose pulled out his pistol and aimed it at Dina but the leader held his arm out forcing him to lower his gun.

"Shoot him instead, he's too dangerous to leave alive," he said while pointing at Dave.

Dina screamed, "No!"

As he squeezed the trigger. The gun fired, sending the bullet towards Dave's temple as his limp body laid on the floor. A small patch of black armor appeared on the surface deflecting the bullet off and striking the one who fired in the head killing him instantly. Dave's eyes opened and he let out a subtle, "Finally."

Dave's body lifted off the ground and turned into a whirlwind of blades in the same motion killing another two of the men. Dina took cover behind a nearby wall as blood sprayed in all directions coating the white walls, floor, and ceiling of the hallway. The mercenary who wasn't in Xenoscale dropped his gun and said, "Fuck this."

He turned and ran back down the hallway, leaving the more advanced mercenary behind. The mercenary aimed his gun at Dave and pulled the trigger, but Dave quickly backflipped and kicked the gun's barrel into the air as it fired harmlessly into the ceiling. With lightning-fast reflexes, Dave lunged forward and stabbed the mercenary up under his helmet. The mercenary's body slumped to the floor with a sickening, lifeless thud. One of the men who had continued forward looked back and watched in horror as his comrade's body hit the floor.

"Shit! Alpha team is down!" he yelled, signaling to the other three to turn around and open fire on Dave. Despite being struck by several bullets, Dave's black scale exterior protected him from harm, and he sprinted forward, dodging the large blasts from the more advanced weapon fired by the second Xenoscale mercenary. As he rushed forward, Dave extended his arms, which transformed into two long blades that spanned the length of the hallway. With lightning speed and precision, he dove into the group. In one fluid motion, Dave sliced through three of the soldiers, their bodies falling to the floor in halves. The Xenoscale mercenary was flung back into the laboratory where the others were fighting. Dave landed gracefully inside the laboratory, his eyes immediately locking onto Thetor attacking Jack. Thetor was on top of Jack, raining down punches on his face. Z was holding onto Thetor from behind, attempting to bite his neck.

Z spotted Dave and called out to him excitedly.

"Dave, you're alive!"

Suddenly, Dave launched forward with a powerful kick, sending Thetor off of Jack and hurtling through the air. After landing, Dave - or rather, his Synthron - turned towards Jack and Z and introduced herself.

"Nice to officially meet you. I'm Lacey, Dave's Synthron. I'll be in control until he regains consciousness."

Next, she turned her attention to a rising mercenary, quickly launching herself at him and sending him flying through the wall.

Jack blinked in surprise and asked, "Lacey?"

Dave gripped the mercenary by the neck with one arm while striking him in the stomach with the other. As he held him, he turned towards Jack.

"Yes, named after Lacey Baker who is the best female skateboarder from Florida. She's won major competitions like the X Games, the Copenhagen Pro, and the Tampa Pro," he explained.

With a swift motion, Dave twisted, snapping the mercenary's neck. The mercenary's legs buckled, and he collapsed against the wall.

Just then, Dina burst into the room, clad in the Xenoscale armor of the fallen mercenary, sans the helmet. In her hand, she carried an advanced weapon. The others gaped at her in surprise. Her eyes sparkled with rage, but she quickly composed herself and asked, "Where's Thetor?"

Jack, Dave, and Z turned to look at the hole in the wall, where they saw Thetor just beginning to stand up. Dina rushed over, shouting, "Motherfucker!"

As she fired large blasts in his direction. He dodged several and realized he was outnumbered and dove through the adjacent wall to strategically retreat. Z yelled, "We can't let him escape, let's cut him off."

All four of them burst out of the lab. Z quickly grabbed the fanny pack containing the vials, and they all took off down the long hallway as fast as they could.

Jack turned to Dina, "Where is Sampson?"

Dina answered as they ran, "Thetor killed him."

As they ran, Dave and Jack quickly pulled ahead of Z and Dina, who were lagging behind. Z, being short and Dina not having a Synthron like the others, struggled to keep up. Jack noticed the widening gap between them and the others and turned his head to look back.

Z shouted ahead to them, his voice straining with exertion, "Don't wait for us, stop him!"

Jack shouted back at them, "Go destroy the beacon!"

Jack's focus returned to the task at hand, and he picked up his pace even more. His heart pounded in his chest as he raced towards the escaping target.

Already at the front of the tunnel, Thetor stood among the remaining mercenaries, his eyes scanning the area for any signs of movement from inside. The two large trucks with mounted turrets had been strategically placed to block the entrance, with their guns aimed towards the tunnel. The soldiers, equipped with advanced weapons and Xenoscale armor, had taken up defensive positions around the area, ready to take on any potential threat. Thetor, looking determined and focused, was directing the units with ease, telling them where to position themselves to prevent any escape. Just as he was about to give another order, Dr. Slotin approached him. Thetor's expression hardened at the sight of the scientist.

"Make sure the beacon is safe," Thetor said firmly, "I'll stay here and ensure they don't escape. There is only one way in and out."

Dr. Slotin, seemingly unfazed by Thetor's imposing presence, quickly assessed the situation and pointed to a group of mercenaries who were standing off to the side.

"Come with me," he ordered firmly, his tone leaving no room for objections. The group immediately sprang into action and began jogging down the tunnel towards the beacon, weapons at the ready. As they ran, two of the mercenaries began to exchange words with each other, their voices barely audible over the sound of their boots thudding against the metal floor.

"Shouldn't this guy be evacuating? He's not a PMC," one of the mercenaries questioned, his voice tinged with uncertainty. The other shrugged.

"I don't know, man. We just do what we're told."

Resolute, they refocused on their mission and pushed forward, aiming to secure the beacon at all costs.

In contrast, Thetor stood vigilant, his hawkish gaze trained on the tunnel's interior. The mercenaries alongside him held their positions in taut silence, their weapons pointed at the tunnel, primed for any sign of movement. Jack and Dave's sudden appearance from a side door of the tunnel seized Thetor's attention.

"Fire!" Thetor commanded.

In response, the mercenaries discharged a barrage of bullets and advanced weapon fire. Their destructive rain pelted everything in its path, from supply crates to parked cars, sparking fires that rapidly spread across the area. The thunderous boom of explosions echoed through the tunnel, drowning out all other sounds.

Thetor rose, signaling frantically for the mercenaries to hold their fire. A few more shots rang out before his shout - "I said hold fire, dammit!" - penetrated the chaos. Frustration laced his voice. Silence eventually fell, leaving the tunnel veiled in smoke and flickering fires.

Just as Thetor and his men took in the destruction, a sudden attack sent one of them crumpling to the ground. In the ensuing surprise, Jack and Dave darted from the smoky haze, moving with electrifying speed. They vaulted over a concrete barrier and infiltrated enemy lines. Wild shots from the rattled mercenaries missed their targets and hit their comrades instead, adding to the chaos.

Jack and Dave cut a swathe through the confusion, neutralizing several soldiers. Thetor, witnessing his men fall one by one, knew he had to intervene. He lunged into the turmoil, but Jack and Dave's cohesive teamwork enabled them to evade him and eliminate the remaining mercenaries who had not already fled in fear.

After clearing their opposition, Jack and Dave sought cover behind a large truck to regroup.

"50% motor units remaining Jack. You're doing good."

Jack smiled and turned to Dave, "Okay Dave we can take him, let's just stick together."

Dave turned his head towards Jack as his back rested against the large truck.

"I'm Lacey, Dave is still unconscious."

Jack shook his head, "Oh ya, sorry."

The pair heard a loud thud above them as Thetor jumped on top of the truck and looked down at them. Jack and Dave both looked up as Thetor's fully armored figure cast a shadow down on them with his arms formed into two large axes.

Meanwhile Dr. Slotin frantically plugged wires and tubes into the beacon while the mercenaries guarded the door. The door was blasted open and the group began to fire at the large opening. Dr. Slotin ignored the commotion and frantically climbed all over various parts of the sphere to try and complete its construction. Dina was outside of the room and fired in hitting one of the men in the chest. She was shot in the leg and it flung her to the ground but when she looked down the armor had protected her.

Z opened the bag and looked at the vials, he turned to Dina, "Listen, these need to be detonated at all costs. If I'm injured, you're going to need to do it."

Dina looked at Z with a confused look, to her the words sounded like a series of clicks and squeals, "I can't understand you!"

Dina yelled as blasts rained around them. Z realized at that moment that Dina had no Synthron implant to communicate with him. He wondered how they could have forgotten this when they split up. He watched as she fired blindly over her cover, drawing the attention of the enemy. He slapped his face in frustration and leaped upward over the cover. He clung to the ceiling for a split second, then launched himself at the group. They looked up and aimed their guns, but he was already on them. He slashed at the less armored men first then ripped the guns out of the two Xenoscale soldiers. Dina blindly fired once more, almost hitting Z.

He turned and yelled, "Hey, watch it!" But all she heard was a loud screech.

She understood what it meant and yelled back, "Sorry!"

Dr. Slotin ran to a terminal on top of a catwalk above the spherical beacon and began typing wildly. Dina saw this and pointed upwards at him yelling, "Look up!"

Z leaped up to the platform, where Dr. Slotin was frantically pressing a button. Z saw two large tanks at the back of the room draining their contents into the sphere. Dr. Slotin slammed his fist into the terminal, effectively disabling it. Retreating from Z, fear spread across his face. Stumbling, he fell to the floor. Above him, Z, though small in size, seemed to loom large.

Through the steel mesh of the catwalk, Z could see the sphere glowing and humming louder and louder. He felt a surge of rage and swung his hand at Dr. Slotin's face, but his blow had no effect. Dr. Slotin's expression changed from terror to a wicked grin as he looked up at Z. Dr. Slotins arms turned black and two large blades shot out of them striking Z in the midsection. He was caught off guard, that section of his body was not armored. Z fell to the ground and held his stomach as the two large gnashes began to bleed. Dr. Slotin stood up and armored his body as he walked towards Z to finish him off, "Surprised?"

Dina from the ground saw this and without hesitation aimed her weapon and fired. The blast hit the catwalk sending one end crashing to the ground. Dr. Slotin launched backwards, landing on the catwalk that wrapped around the edge of the room, while Z tumbled down the slope. Dina ran over to him and slid next to his injured body. The hum from the sphere increased as she knelt beside him. Z lifted his head and saw the large tanks were already halfway emptied. Grabbing two vials from his fanny pack, Z twisted them together as his purple blood pooled around him. Dina watched the unsettling scene, her eyes shifting from Z's large wounds back to his face.

"Just tell me what to do," she implored, mustering every bit of her composure.

Z, although lacking the ability to communicate verbally in English, understood enough to convey a crucial message. Dipping a finger in his own blood, he scrawled a chilling command on the wall beside him: "RUN".

Next, he activated the device. A digital timer blinked to life, displaying characters in an alien language, and the countdown began.

Dina glanced between the cryptic numbers and Z's warning. Realization dawned that Z had activated a bomb and was unlikely to survive his injuries. She sprung to her feet, racing towards the door. Noticing her escape, Dr. Slotin leaped down from the catwalk and began sprinting after her.

As soon as Dina exited the room, she spun around, positioning her gun towards the door. The moment Dr. Slotin appeared, she fired, sending him hurtling back into the room. Without wasting another second, Dina pivoted and ran towards the tunnel's exit.

At the tunnel's entrance, Dave held a firm grip on Thetor from behind, inhibiting his movements. Meanwhile, Jack launched a series of powerful punches at Thetor's armored stomach. Each blow sent shards of black crystals and dust scattering into the air. The evident damage to Thetor's armor and dwindling units suggested that Jack's onslaught was effective.

Spotting a brief opportunity, Thetor gathered his strength and broke free from Dave's grasp. In a swift counterattack, he unleashed a powerful kick that hit Jack square in the chest. The impact sent Jack hurtling backward, he smashed into a nearby truck with a loud crash. Thetor's kick not only sent Jack flying but also flung Thetor and Dave out of the tunnel entrance. They tumbled down the steep hillside, bodies clashing against the rough terrain as they wrestled with each other.

Jack, regaining his bearings, clambered to his feet and sprinted towards the tunnel's exit. Straining his eyes against the dense foliage and night's darkness, he tried to spot Dave or Thetor. Suddenly, the sounds of blasts reverberated from behind him. He whipped his head around to see Dina shooting backwards as she ran, her voice ringing with urgency as she shouted, "Bomb!"

He scanned the tunnel for Z but found no sign of him. Jack's heart pounded as he realized that the vials had been mixed and time was ticking. He cast another look down the hill to see Thetor and Dave still locked in their fierce battle.

"Where's Z?" Jack called out, his voice edged with concern. But Dina was solely focused on the impending disaster and ignored his question.

Resolved to find and save Z, Jack turned to dash into the tunnel, only to find himself suddenly unable to move.

"Jack, I'm sorry, but I cannot allow you to do that," Nexo's voice resonated loudly in his mind.

Overwhelmed with frustration and panic, Jack protested, "Nexo, let me go! This is my body!" His voice echoed with defiance.

"I'm sorry, Jack, but if you enter that tunnel, your odds of survival are near zero. You must seek shelter from the blast immediately," came the calm reply, Jack's body remained under unyielding control.

Jack's struggle against Nexo persisted, a desperate attempt to reclaim his own movements. But it was already too late.

Dina had swiftly reached Jack at the hill's edge, the danger awaiting them inside the tunnel evident. With no hesitation, she charged at him, forcefully tackling him. Their bodies intertwined as they cascaded down the slope, colliding with unforgiving trees and rocks. Each impact sent sharp jolts of pain coursing through both Jack and Dina.

Finally, their tumbling journey halted, landing them close to where Dave and Thetor's intense fight continued. Thetor, gaining the upper hand, was on top of Dave, launching punches at his face.

Jack groaned, pain radiating from his battered body as he forced his head to lift. His gaze was drawn upward to the imposing mountain looming over them.

Suddenly, an explosion of unimaginable magnitude shook the surroundings, causing the mountain to appear as if it were lifting itself before violently ejecting an enormous plume of debris in all directions. In an instant, the tunnel and everything inside it were obliterated, consumed by the cataclysmic blast. The sheer power of the explosion incinerated all within its reach, leaving nothing but a swirling cloud of black soot that rose ominously into the sky. The top of the mountain was blown clean off, leaving a massive, gaping wound in the once-pristine landscape.

The impact of the explosion propelled Jack, Dina, Thctor, and Dave through the air like weightless pieces of paper, their bodies helplessly flung in different directions. They tumbled and spun, each at the mercy of the shockwave, as they were scattered and disoriented.

CHAPTER 19 - THE KNIFE

The moonlight peeked through the blackened trees, casting a healing glow on Jack's soot covered face.

"Jack get up," Nexo's voice spoke softly as Jack opened one eye, *"Jack, you need to get up."*

Jack coughed as he tried to sit up.

"Jack, you have 5% units left."

Scanning his surroundings, Jack spotted Dina's body about ten feet away, lying motionless and covered in black soot and ash. Dave and Thetor were nowhere in sight.

Dragging himself over to Dina, Jack gave her a gentle shake. "Dina, get up," he urged. Reaching down, he checked for a pulse.

Upon feeling a faint but steady rhythm, a wave of relief washed over him.

Squinting through the dense foliage, he caught a glimpse of distant streetlights, their glow piercing through the canopy. Determined to find Dave, he carefully lifted Dina's unconscious body and began dragging her towards the nearby road. When he arrived at the roadside, Jack gently leaned Dina against a sturdy guardrail post.

Lifting himself over the guardrail, Jack surveyed the desolate road stretching out before him. The pavement, devoid of any life, was blanketed by a thin layer of ash, lending it an eerie resemblance to a soft blanket of freshly fallen snow.

Ash from the explosion still trickled down from the sky. While Jack was taking stock of their surroundings, the sound of rapid footsteps approaching from behind broke the silence.

Startled, he swiftly turned, only to see Thetor leaping over the guardrail towards him with astounding agility. Caught off guard, Jack stumbled backward. As he landed on the ground, the ash gently dispersed, creating a soft cloud around him. Thetor, undeterred by Jack's stumble, gracefully touched down on the pavement, his movements leaving behind elegant streaks in the layer of ash as he slid across the ground. Jack stood up and found himself face to face with Thetor on the desolate ash covered road. The yellow street lights showed that Thetor's armor was only covering key areas, Jack knew he was weak. Thetor walked forward, his eyes fixed on Jack. A menacing smirk played across

Thetor's lips as he spoke, his voice dripping with a cold, calculated intimidation.

"Jack," Thetor's tone was laced with the knowledge of their past encounters, "You've proven to be no match for my superior capabilities. I've defeated you before, and this time will be no different."

His words were designed to instill fear and doubt within Jack. The memory of their previous confrontations lingered, serving as a constant reminder of Thetor's superiority.

"Omega is a force that cannot be overcome. Surrender now, and perhaps your consciousness can ascend before your body expires."

Jack's gaze shifted to the smoldering mountain, he thought of Z as he watched the raging fire. An overwhelming surge of anger consumed him. In a flash, Jack sprinted towards Thetor, his bladed hand ready to strike. With a thunderous roar, he shouted at his adversary, "The only one expiring today is you!"

Thetor's armor disappeared as he formed his hand into a blade also. The two met and the clash of blades reverberated through the air as Thetor and Jack engaged in a fierce duel. Their weapons clashed repeatedly, a symphony of metal meeting metal. With each collision, sparks illuminated their faces and black shards were sent flying. Gradually each of their blades shrank as they clashed together until both were left without any motor units, leaving them defenseless and exposed. Jack's energy dwindled rapidly, he felt his strength leave his body. Thetor kicked Jack backwards but it only staggered him slightly. Nexo's voice resonated in his mind.

"Jack, you're at 0%. I can't help you any longer."

Thetor looked down at his human hands then looked back up at Jack, "Looks like we have to finish this the old fashion way."

Thetor and Jack confronted each other, exchanging a series of punches. One of Thetor's blows caught Jack off guard, momentarily dazing him, but he quickly shook it off and tackled Thetor, forcing him to the ground. Mounting Thetor's chest, Jack relentlessly delivered a barrage of punches to his face, causing his head to rebound off the pavement with each strike.

Determined to defend himself, Thetor reached down, retrieving a knife from his boot, and pressed it against Jack's throat. Reacting swiftly, Jack grabbed hold of Thetor's wrist, preventing him from slashing his neck, and they wrestled, eventually rolling over so that Thetor found himself on top. He spun the blade in his hand and pointed the knife's tip at Jack's chest, Thetor began to drive it downward. Jack, mustering every ounce of strength, desperately employed both hands to halt the knife's progress, inch by inch. Despite his efforts, the blade managed to break through the skin of Jack's chest, but he summoned even more strength and managed to lift the blade away. A grimace formed on Jack's face as he furrowed his brows and clenched his teeth, his gaze meeting Thetor's emotionless eyes. But suddenly Jack felt Thetor's strength eased.

He blinked several times as if awakening from a trance. Thetor looked down at Jack, "What's up creampuff?"

Jack looked confused as he continued to hold the knife up, "Franklin?" Jack uttered, his voice tinged with uncertainty.

Suddenly, Thetor's voice shifted, the tone was softer, more human. It was unmistakably Franklin's voice that filled the air. He spoke with an impending finality, "I don't have much time, Jack. But I need you to know - I'm sorry, for everything."

With deliberate intent, Thetor adjusted his position, aligning the blade's point towards his own chest. Jack's hands remained rigid on the handle, a silent witness to the impending act. Then, in a decisive movement, Thetor surrendered to gravity. He drove himself downwards with an unflinching resolve, the blade puncturing his heart in a fatal embrace.

Underneath Thetor's now diseased body, Jack laid pinned against the ground. A mixture of emotions washed over Jack as he absorbed the weight and stillness of his fallen opponent.

With tear-filled eyes, Jack lifted his gaze upwards, as if seeking solace from the star filled sky above. The soft hum of the yellow streetlights filled the air, creating a serene ambiance amidst the aftermath of chaos. Jack's thoughts were interrupted by a congratulatory message from Nexo.

"Jack, you did it."

Feeling a mix of exhaustion and relief, Jack gently rolled Thetor's lifeless body off his own, taking a moment to collect himself. He breathed deeply, wiping away tears that had escaped during the intense battle. As he sat up, the distant wail of sirens reached his ears, a sign that the magnitude of the explosion had not gone unnoticed. The sound reawakened Jack's determination, pushing him to his feet.

"Jack, your sister, she still has the enemy Synthron," Nexo's voice was laced with a hint of urgency. Jack looked back to where he had left Dina. "You're right."

"We need to get her back to the ship, now."

With renewed purpose, Jack swiftly made his way back to where his sister was propped up against the guardrail. He carefully positioned himself behind her, gripping her under the arms, and began to walk backward, dragging her limp body along the ash-laden ground. A faint trail marked their progress. In the periphery of his vision, he caught sight of someone, and a flicker of concern tinged his emotions. He turned to see Dave standing in the middle of the road, wearing a perplexed expression. Dave, noticing Jack dragging Dina's unconscious form, hurried over to them, passing Thetor's body as he jogged over, his confusion evident.

"Jack, what are we doing out here? What happened?" Dave questioned, trying to make sense of the situation. A smile graced Jack's face, relieved to see his friend unharmed. He replied, his voice filled with a mix of gratitude and amusement.

"Good to see you back, Dave. I met Lacey. Help me get Dina back to the ship," Jack said with a relieved smile, emphasizing the return of Dave's true self. Dave's face had a hint of embarrassment, he grabbed Dina's legs and began to help move her.

"You've met Lacey, right? Yeah, I told her that if I ever pass out, she's in charge," Dave reminded himself.

"Hang on, what went down? And where's Z?"

Concern filled his eyes as he began to look around at the scene. Jack looked up at Dave as the pair carried Dina off the road and began to climb the hill up to the ship.

"Just help me get her back to the ship, and I'll explain everything."

Jack and Dave trudged up the hill, their ascent becoming arduous without the enhanced strength provided by their Synthrons. After climbing halfway heavily breathing, Jack paused, and carefully lowered Dina to the ground.

"Let's take a break. Once we're back at the ship, I'm going to chug a gallon of that plastic shit," Jack said, a touch of exhaustion evident in his voice. Dave chuckled, his own fatigue apparent.

"Yeah, I've got about 1% of motor units left. That must have been one rad explosion, kinda pissed I missed it."

The pair glanced down the hill, observing the rows of fire trucks and police cars that had arrived at the scene. The authorities had caution-taped off the area, beginning their investigation into the catastrophic event. Dina groaned as she lay on the ground, nursing her throbbing head.

"Ow, my damn head," she muttered in discomfort.

Jack kneeled beside her, "Hang in there, Dina. We'll get you back to the ship."

Dina sat up, and suddenly clutched her ears, wincing in pain. Confusion etched across Jack's face as he tried to understand her reaction. "Dina, are you alright? We need to—"

Dina interrupted, her voice strained, "Why won't you shut up?"

Jack stood up, baffled by her response. Dina continued as she grabbed her head, her tone filled with urgency, "You have to stop talking!"

"Jack the enemy Synthron is almost fully integrated. We should ensure that doesn't happen."

"No!" Jack exclaimed, defiance evident in his voice. Turning to Dave, he urgently instructed, "We need to get her to the ship. Help me carry her."

With one arm draped over Jack's shoulders and another supporting Dina, they hoisted her up, determination fueling their movements. They sprinted up the hill, stumbling over uneven terrain as they raced through the darkened forest.

"Jack, I estimate you have less than ten minutes. If she becomes fully assimilated, she'll possess the strength of a complete Synthron and she'll kill both of you within seconds."

Ignoring Nexo's words, Jack pressed on, his focus solely on reaching the safety of the ship. Soon, they emerged from the forest and entered the open field atop the hill. The moonlight cast a pale glow on the swaying grass as a gentle breeze swept through.

Finally, they reached the ship and gently laid Dina down on the central bed. Jack and Dave stood by her side, their eyes filled with concern as they watched her writhe atop the bed, clearly in distress.

"Nexo, you said we could save her. How?" Jack implored, his voice laced with desperation.

"At this stage, it may be too late. You need to provide her with a friendly Synthron. Your motor units have completely depleted, but perhaps Dave still has some remaining. He must load a sample into the machine, and it should initiate the process automatically."

Jack looked up at Dave, a glimmer of hope in his eyes. "You need to give her a Synthron, just like you did for me."

Dave turned around, his movements resolute as he loaded the machine with the last 1% of motor units he possessed. As he worked, Nexo explained, *"Jack, I'd say there's about a fifty-fifty chance of this working. We need a plan B if it fails."*

Jack glanced towards the back of the ship, contemplating his options. With determination, he walked over to the compartment holding the vials of fuel. Carefully, he picked up one vial of each kind and retrieved the connector designed to join them together. Placing the two vials side by side, he screwed the connector securely between them, ensuring that he did not activate the detonation button just yet.

"If she turns, I'll detonate the ship. I won't be strong enough to fight her, but she won't survive this," Jack declared, his voice resolute.

"This plan is risky, and I must advise against it."

Jack retorted, his frustration palpable, "Just like you advised me at the tunnel."

Nexo conceded, acknowledging Jack's point. *"We will discuss that, Jack. I understand your concern."*

Returning to Dave, who had finished setting up the machine, Jack posed the question, "Now what?"

Dave looked up, his expression determined, "I think we need to stand back, and... do this." With a swift motion, Dave unlatched the front of Dina's armor, removing the chest plate and placing it against the nearby wall. He leaned over Dina, gently lifting her shirt to expose her belly button. Stepping back, he motioned for Jack to do the same.

The machine sprang into action, the internal lights of the ship turned blue to indicate readiness. An arm emerged from the wall, equipped with a needle. The gray-black solution flowed into the needle, which was then inserted into Dina's stomach. After the fluid entered her body, the arm retracted, and the blue light within the ship transitioned to green. The ship resonated with an audible chime, signifying the completion of the process.

Jack looked down at Dina, "That felt way longer when I did it," he remarked, recalling his own experience.

Dave glanced across the table, a slight smirk forming on his face.

"Well, you were also extremely high," Dave replied, a hint of amusement in his voice. Jack kept a close watch on Dina, hoping for any signs of improvement.

"How long, Nexo?" Jack inquired, seeking answers.

"Her body is already loaded with the enemy Synthron, so the integration won't take as long. Maybe fifteen minutes. The hope is that what we just injected will be able to hijack the hardware already installed."

Jack's finger gently caressed the button of the explosive, ensuring he was prepared for any potential trouble. He turned to Dave, who was nervously observing the unfolding scene.

"Dave, you don't have to stay. There's no point in both of us blowing up if this goes bad," Jack said, his voice filled with concern. Dave turned to face Jack, his gaze unwavering.

"You just want me to miss out on both explosions, huh? Nice try. But I'm not going anywhere," Dave replied, his resolve clear. Jack and Dave took their seats, facing Dina. They both grabbed the plastic solution and took small sips, their faces scrunching up at the taste. Dave chuckled, teasing Jack about his earlier statement.

"What happened to chugging a gallon?" Dave joked.

"Fuck off," Jack retorted, a slight smile tugging at the corners of his lips. They waited in silence, hoping for a sign of life from Dina. She lay still on the bed, unconscious. Dave glanced at the time on his phone. It had been several minutes since the injection.

255

He could not stand the suspense any longer. He turned to Jack and asked, "What happened to Z?"

Jack's eyes stayed fixed on Dina's body as he answered, "I don't know. Dina was with him, but he didn't make it out before the explosion."

Dave stood up, "Do you think he's alive? Maybe we should search for him."

Jack shook his head, "No, we shouldn't, I saw the blast. It was huge. Nobody could have survived that. Also the tunnel collapsed and the whole area is crawling with cops and firefighters now. There's no point in looking for him."

Dave felt a surge of grief and anger. He clenched his fists and sat back down next to Jack. He wished he could do something but all he could do was sit and watch Dina's chest rise and fall.

CHAPTER 20 - THE SUITS

The ship's interior was bathed in a soothing green light that reflected on Dina's tired face. She stirred and let out a moan. The smell of melted plastic and sweat assaulted her nostrils as she opened her eyes. She saw her brother sitting next to her, his hand on the detonator. Dina lifted her head slightly and said in a flat voice, "Hello, brother."

Jack smiled and released his grip on the button, "Dina."

Dave, who had been dozing off next to him, jerked awake with a gasp, "Is it Dina?"

He looked around and saw Dina and Jack embracing and realized it was true. As Dina wrapped her arms around Jack, she was still adjusting to the effects of the Synthron. She squeezed him harder than she meant to and Jack winced, "Too tight."

Dina loosened her grip, "Oh sorry."

Dina took in their surroundings, her gaze wide with awe as she asked, "Where are we?"

Jack simply smiled in response, not offering any verbal answer. He then started walking towards the back of the ship, leaving Dina to her observations. As she looked around, realization dawned on her.

"So this is the asset everyone was so concerned with," she murmured, more to herself than to Jack.

"Yep," Jack confirmed, his attention on a drawer he was opening. Inside, he carefully returned the vials to their slots, then shut the drawer, leaving no hint of the compartment's existence.

Dina, meanwhile, rose from the bed and started inspecting their surroundings more closely. She reached out to touch the walls of the ship, appreciating the intricate design. "Wow, now this is interesting," she remarked.

Jack turned to face her, his curiosity piqued. "What's interesting?"

"This," she said, her fingers tracing the patterns on the wall, "is the same building style used for the beacon."

Dave, who had quietly followed them, couldn't help but gasp. "You made a beacon!"

"We blew it up, don't worry," Jack assured him, shaking his head. "That's one of the things you missed." Then, turning back to Dina, he added, "Also Dina, I was wondering how you built it so fast."

Dina peeled off the armor and stacked the pieces on top of the chest plate, creating a neat pile. She answered them with a serious tone. "We didn't build it. We found it. Thetor just gave us the instructions we needed to get it working. He had convinced The Director it was an advanced energy reactor and could solve humanity's energy problems."

Jack returned to Dave and sat down, confused. "Where did you find it? That doesn't make any sense."

Dina shrugged. "I don't know. It was one of the few assets we acquired that had a classified history."

Jack frowned as he asked, "How often did that happen?"

"Rarely. The beacon was one of them, and the other was the source of Xenoscale," Dina said as she gestured to the heap of armor she had shaped on the ground. She picked up a piece and compared it with the ship. The design was almost identical, but the materials were different.

"Someone using technology from The Creators must have come to Earth before."

Jack asked Dina, "Is there any way to trace the origin of the beacon?"

Dina shook her head, "Jack, they just tried to kill me and then we destroyed one of their biggest caches of alien tech. We're not exactly on friendly terms right now."

"I suppose you're right."

Dave looked at them both, "Okay, you guys need to fill me in on what happened there."

Over the next hour, Jack and Dina detailed the events that transpired within the tunnel. They shared their individual perspectives, weaving together a story that helped form a complete picture.

When Dina mentioned the moment Z was stabbed by Dr. Slotin, Jack visibly gasped. "Hold on, hold on, hold on," he interrupted, "what do you mean Dr. Slotin was a Synthron?"

Dina simply nodded in affirmation, recounting, "Yeah, after he triggered the beacon, Z approached him. Then Dr. Slotin transformed - he looked like one of you. His arms became long black metal blades and when I shot at him, he just armored up."

Jack furrowed his brows, his mind racing to comprehend the new information. "This makes no sense," he confessed, struggling to piece together the puzzle.

"My records indicate that sometimes enemy Synthrons don't take over a host right away after integration but stay dormant."

Dina cast a glance around the ship, her gaze falling on the scattered dirty clothes and discarded food that littered the floor. "What doesn't make sense is the state of this ship. It's disgusting," she remarked.

Standing, she began to walk towards the exit. "In fact, I could use some fresh air."

Dave and Jack exchanged embarrassed glances. As Dina left the ship, Dave quickly got to his feet and trailed after her. "Sorry for the mess," he apologized. "We weren't expecting any visitors."

Jack followed suit, unconsciously wiping his hands on his pants as he did so. "Yeah, it's been a while since we cleaned up," he admitted.

Once they stepped outside, the trio's attention was immediately drawn to the distant flashing lights of emergency vehicles. Jack turned towards Dina and Dave, proposing, "Want to go see what's going on?"

Their response was a unanimous nod and a joint, "Sure." Together, they walked over to a hill, securing a vantage point where they could oversee the unfolding scene.

The intensity of the flames was diminishing, and the police had extended their safety perimeter, deploying more caution tape and erecting additional road barriers around the affected area. A crowd of cops and firefighters surrounded Thetor's body, staring at his metal jaw in disbelief. It was unlike anything they had ever encountered. A senior detective was on the phone with someone higher up while another one showed him one of the futuristic weapons that the Xenoscale soldiers had used. They also noticed the mercenary that Jack and Z had tied up being escorted by the police in his underwear.

Jack let out a chuckle. "Look, he made it out alive."

Dave squinted in the direction Jack was looking. "Who's that?" he asked.

In response, Jack gestured to the uniform he was wearing, one he had stolen earlier. "It's his," he explained.

They continued to observe from their hilltop perch as three black SUVs sped down the road, halting at the police barrier. They were waved through and parked near Thetor's body. Several men in black suits got out, one of them knelt down next to him for a moment, then got up and made a gesture with his finger, telling the others to clear the area. The men in black suits went around and ordered everyone to leave at once.

Some of the police argued, but eventually they all complied. The area was soon empty except for these men in black suits. One of them pointed at the hill and a spotlight shone towards Jack, Dina, and Dave. They quickly ducked under a bush as the light swept over them. Jack whispered. "Time to go, guys. Let's get out of here."

They crawled backwards and ran back to the ship. As Dina approached the ship she said, "Wait, why does it look like a big rock?"

Jack ushered her onboard, "Get in and I'll show you."

Jack sat down on the small seat where Z used to sit. As he sat down, Z's seat morphed into a large captain's chair that fit Jack's frame perfectly. Dave and Dina sat behind Jack. They nervously watched as he reached down for the controls, "I watched Z fly so I think I can do it."

"Jack, you have me, remember? You'll know how to fly it."

Jack pushed a few buttons and grabbed the controls. The ship lifted off the ground and soared into the sky. The Luxastra shot up vertically, but the passengers barely felt any G-forces as it broke through the clouds and reached low Earth-orbit. The sun was rising over the horizon of the planet. Dave and Dina got up and admired the view. Jack looked back at them.

"So, where do you want to go?"

EPILOGUE

In the weeks following the devastating tunnel explosion, the massive corporation known as Advanced Acquisition crumbled, its fragments shattered and enveloped by other companies. Despite their tenacity, Jack and his comrades could not unmask the elusive men in black, but the extent of their influence became disturbingly clear. The incident was concealed masterfully, with the media obediently spinning a gas leak narrative, pulling the public's attention away from the unsettling truth. The Director resisted the dissolving of the company vehemently, but fate had other plans. Shortly after expressing his opposition publicly, The Director met a tragic end during a late-night assault, reported as a botched mugging.

Despite the relentless efforts of online conspiracy groups, who painstakingly dissected inconsistencies and leaked images of the

Xenoscale, their revelations were largely dismissed as fabricated hoaxes or props from a movie by a world kept in the dark.

Jack, Dina, and Dave paid tribute to Z in a quiet, personal ceremony. Despite feeling that Z deserved much grander recognition for his Earth-saving heroism, they understood his legacy would persist only in the hearts of those lucky enough to know him well.

As three months slipped away like sand through an hourglass, Jack, driven by an unquenchable thirst for knowledge, resolved to return to academia. While he knew that with Nexo, formal education was not necessary, he felt he needed it for personal growth and fulfillment. Leaving behind his modest apartment and mundane job, Jack wholeheartedly embraced the life of a full-time student, during the fall semester. His chess skills, significantly amplified by Nexo's capabilities, earned him a prestigious scholarship, granting him access to a world of intellectual exploration and limitless possibilities. With Nexo as his companion, Jack honed his abilities and broadened his understanding of the universe. Together, they embarked on an exciting journey of self-discovery and academic pursuit, Jack's curiosity driving him to unravel the mysteries of the cosmos and deepen his understanding of Synthron technology.

While Jack's focus remained primarily on his research, his friend Dave continued to channel his passion for skateboarding. Dave ventured to the sunny shores of Florida, where he eagerly prepared to compete in a thrilling skateboarding competition that would push his skills to new heights. He also had a bit of extra time for surfing. Determined to embrace a fair playing field, he made sure to deactivate the aid of his Synthrons, although Lacey's guidance still lingered in the depths of his consciousness. The palm-fringed beaches and vibrant skateboarding community of Florida welcomed Dave with open arms, igniting his spirit and fostering new connections. Here, he would carve his own path, pushing the boundaries of his craft and savoring every exhilarating moment.

Meanwhile, Dina, disillusioned with the corporate world following the disintegration of her former company, yearned for a different path. She longed for a life infused with joy, freedom, and the soothing embrace of a seaside paradise. Empowered by her financial prudence, she decided to join Dave in Florida. Utilizing her hard-earned savings, she transformed her aspirations into reality by opening a lively beach bar appropriately named 'The Water Cooler.' It was a vibrant sanctuary where locals and tourists alike could bask in the sun-drenched ambiance, savor refreshing cocktails, and create cherished memories.

Dina's beach bar became a beloved hotspot, adorned with vibrant umbrellas, swaying hammocks, and the gentle melody of waves crashing against the shore. Patrons reveled in the carefree atmosphere, relishing in the delicious concoctions crafted with Dina's passion and expertise. And there, amidst the palm trees and flow of the tides, an old, rusted-out, sun-bleached bus stood parked out front, an unexpected yet whimsical addition to the coastal scenery. The bus, despite its dilapidated appearance, would vanish from time to time. One of these times was when Jack was on his Thanksgiving break from university and visiting his parents at home.

Jack was sitting in his childhood bedroom, surrounded by remnants of his past, lost in a daydream about Thetor's final words. His thoughts were abruptly interrupted by the distinct clink of a pebble striking his window. He initially brushed it off, assuming it was nothing more than a random noise. But when the sound repeated itself, curiosity got the best of him. Opening the window, he peered outside, to find Dina and Dave standing by the side of the house, sharing a hearty laugh. Looking down at them, Jack could not help but wear a concerned expression.

"Dina, you're going to wake up Mom and Dad," he whispered, trying to maintain a sense of responsibility. Dina, with her newly acquired sun-kissed glow and carefree spirit, playfully egged Jack on.

"Come on, Jack! You're twenty-five now. Don't be such a pussy!"

Her mischievous grin was contagious, and Dave chimed in with a chuckle, echoing her sentiment. Jack could not resist the temptation, with a burst of spontaneity, he decided to embrace the thrill and go out for a little adventure. He took a leap from the second story window, executing a graceful flip, landing right beside his friends. As his feet touched the ground, a mix of exhilaration and amusement washed over him.

"Okay, you got me up." A grin spread across Jack's face. Dina playfully slapped him on the back.

"Good," she said with a mischievous glint in her eyes.

"It's the day before Thanksgiving, also known as the best day to go to the bar."

The three of them made their way to the only bar in town and secured a cozy booth. They settled in, ready to unwind and enjoy each other's company. Laughter filled the air as they had drinks and exchanged stories about their recent adventures and caught up on what they had been up to for the past few months.

However, their peaceful evening took an unexpected turn when the door of the bar swung open with a loud creak. In walked the gang that Franklin used to do business with, their presence instantly sending an uneasy tension through the air. Scabs, the leader of the gang, noticed Jack sitting in the booth and purposefully strode over, his eyes filled with determination.

"I know you're the one who made Franklin vanish," he growled, his raspy voice laced with anger. "And now, you have to pay."

The atmosphere in the bar grew tense as patrons exchanged anxious glances. Instinctively aware of the imminent clash, some got up and left anxious of what would soon take place. Jack's face hardened, his gaze locked onto Scabs, calculating his next move. Turning to Dina and Dave, a mischievous smile spread across their faces, hinting at their hidden abilities. Scabs brandished a knife, slashing it towards Jack with malicious intent.

"Danger detected."

In a swift motion, Jack's Synthron-enhanced reflexes kicked in, surpassing the capabilities of an ordinary human. He snatched the blade from mid-air, his grip unwavering despite the force behind the attack. Scabs' eyes widened in disbelief, a hint of fear flashing across his face as he recognized the extraordinary skill of his opponent. Jack's gaze brimmed with confidence and amusement. He tightened his grip on the knife, causing it to crumble like a fragile artifact, its remnants scattering to the floor.

Scabs stood frozen, his bravado shattered in an instant. Realizing the futility of their fight, Scabs and the gang members quickly fled the bar, their escape driven by a sudden surge of fear. The bartender, recovering from the unexpected turn of events, looked at Dina.

"We'll settle the bill whenever you're ready," Dina calmly remarked.

The bartender paused for a moment, taking in the astonishing scene, before responding, "Consider it, on the house."

Jack, Dina, and Dave left the bar and talked long into the night until they each began to feel exhausted. Eventually Jack decided to call it a night and went back home.

As he lay in bed, he pondered over his recent accomplishments. Not only had he thwarted the beacon's construction, but he had also managed to realign his life and rebuild bridges with his sister.

Despite all the headway, a nagging sensation in the recesses of his mind remained. The lingering thought that his victories were not wholly his. Without Nexo, none of this would have been feasible, so he should feel gratified. Still, he found himself questioning if he could have made any strides independently.

That was when it hit him – it did not really matter. Nexo was here to stay, for better or worse. Jack's victories would now have to be shared with his Synthron. With that realization, he bid goodnight to his newfound ally and life partner, "Goodnight, Nexo."

"Goodnight, Jack."

ACKNOWLEDGEMENTS

Writing this book has been a significant journey, and there are a few people whose assistance was invaluable along the way.

Firstly, I extend heartfelt thanks to my wife, Jessica. Her continuous support and diligent work as my editor were vital in shaping this book.

My mother also deserves special recognition. Her contributions went beyond the editing process. Her unwavering belief in me and her continuous encouragement were key drivers in this journey.

I would also like to express my gratitude to my wonderful Aunt Traci for giving the book a final edit. Her keen eye for detail and valuable feedback greatly improved the quality of the manuscript.

Lastly, to you, the reader: your support brings this book to life. I hope that the pages within brought you as much joy to read as they brought me to write. Thank you.

74404235R00163